# Messed Up

Janet Nichols Lynch

SCHOLASTIC INC.
New York Toronto London Auckland
Sydney Mexico City New Delhi Hong Kong

*This is a work of fiction. Names, characters, places, and incidents are the product of the author's imagination. Any resemblance to actual events, locales, or persons is coincidental.*

ISBN 978-0-545-38498-8

12 11 10 9 8 7 6 5 4 3 2 1          11 12 13 14 15 16/0

Printed in the U.S.A.          40

First Scholastic printing, September 2011

*To Sean*

## Acknowledgments

I am grateful to my literary agent, Jodie Rhodes, for drawing this novel into the light of publishing, and for my editor, Mary Cash, for her helpful suggestions in shaping the manuscript. Thanks to my running friends, Mary Jo, Richard, Michele, Julie, and Beth, who heard R.D.'s story too many times. As always, I've got my family to thank: Tim, Caitlin, and Sean. Sean, filmmaker extraordinaire, was the first reader of this manuscript, and he offered insightful comments and tremendous enthusiasm for the work. I'm grateful for the camaraderie of my niece Julianne and my colleagues, the teachers of Visalia Unified School District, who teach their hearts out every day. Yes, it's hard; yes, it's fun. And, of course, there are the kids. They're in here, every one of them.

# one

CAT FIGHT—about the only good thing that can happen the first day of school. I'm close to the action, two brown girls going at it. The fat girl has the little girl down on the sidewalk, pinned between her thunder thighs, her butt waving around like some kind of big blue balloon. The little one has a red rubber band thingie in her hair so we all know what it's about. Red for *Norteño*, blue for *Sureño*—these are the colors of my town.

The little one's still got on her big hoop earrings, which means she's the one who got jumped. She's kicking and screaming and shaking her head, trying to keep the other girl from grabbing hold and ripping her lobe clean through. The big one scrapes her long blue fingernails down the little one's face. The little girl's teeth snap once, twice, then clamp down on the fat one's hand. Whoa, chicks fight nasty. Both girls are streaked with the little one's color.

A teacher comes running, yelling, "Stop, stop!" She's new—I never seen her anyways—young, dressed like a student in Capris and a short stretchy top. She grabs the big girl's shoulder and tries to pull her off the little one, but that big mama don't pay no attention. Blue twists red's hair around her fist and jerks her head back like a yo-yo on a string. Kids cheer and yell, "Yeah, get down."

Now this is going to sound crazy, but it's like my mind races ahead to the next minute, and I can see the little girl's head cracked open, blood streaming over the sidewalk. All of a sudden my foot comes up in front of me. I set my shoe up against that big mama's hip and give a shove, way harder than I need to, and that big blue butt goes rolling like a giant bowling ball, whacks against the wall and sort of bounces back and whacks it again. It's so funny everybody hoots and cheers, except for new teacher who got kicked a good one by the big blue mama.

Teacher looks like she's about to pass out, but she keeps doing her teacher thing, straight-arming yo-mama against the wall so little spitfire can scramble out from under her and spring to her feet. She's about to fly into the pinned-down girl's face, but here I go again. My hand flings out like it's attached to someone else's body, grabbing a wad of the back of her shirt.

I'm pretty tall for a Mexican cuz I'm part Cheyenne Indian. I can hold her up so high only her toes touch the ground, like she's bicycling with no bike under her, and all the kids hoot some more. Then I wonder what the hell I'm doing, helping a teacher break up a cat fight and ruining all the fun.

"Hold on to her!" new teacher yells. "Follow me!" By then she's got the big girl up, steering her from behind by the elbows and limping toward the office. She don't even look back, she's so sure I'll do what she sez.

I let go of the little girl's shirt and put my hands on her shoulders. Whoa! She's like sizzling! Her muscles are like jumping and twitching. Every time she takes a breath her whole back ripples like some kind of monster is inside her trying to bust out. It sort of creeps me out, but it's sort of hot too. She's got big boobs, nice and round like apples. I can see over her shoulder down her black shirt. She's wearing a black bra and there's a little red rosebud there, wearing her colors in a secret place, but not so secret cuz of how low-cut the shirt is. We got dress code here at Buzz Middle, no saggin-and-baggin for guys, no spaghetti straps and bare bellies for girls, but still they dress like hoes, then act like they don't know what it does to us guys.

I stick out my chest and haul the little hottie over to the office.

I hear, "Hey! R.D. helped break up the fight."

Thinking quick, I point to the red thingie in the girl's hair and the red stripe on my T-shirt.

Someone sez, "You got a color, R.D., for reals?"

"Dude! R.D. got a color."

I look over at who's talking. Dumb seventh graders—well, now they're eighth graders. I should be a freshman, but I failed. All my homies cept Dominic and Scraps are gone up to the high school, but I'm stuck here, another year at Buzz Middle.

# two

IN THE OFFICE new teacher nods toward one of the rooms off the hall. "In there. Stay with her while I get help." She takes the big girl to another holding tank.

We're in some junk room with filing cabinets and stacked-up old computers, books and half-ate boxes of snack chips. I set the girl in a chair—she isn't gonna run or nothing—and I set down too.

She drops her face in her hands and blubbers. "My sister's gonna whoop my ass." She reaches up in her hair, pulls out the red rubber band thingie, some long black hairs hanging off it, and stuffs it in her pants pocket. She thinks again and drops it in the trash. She should know they check the trash.

New teacher comes back with Mr. Bowan, who looks right at me and sez, "Well, well, R.D. Mitchell, what a surprise." He's funny like that. He looks like Homer Simpson, same bald head and pot belly, only he's black. "Fighting the first day of school. Is this a record, R.D.?"

"Sure is," I sez and give a smirk.

He calls me incorrigible cuz I don't ever learn. "What are your grandparents going to say about this?"

"They won't care."

"They won't care," he repeats, just to make me sound dumb. "How are your grandparents?" Mr. Bowan already been out to the house a couple of times.

"Fine," I sez back real quick, even though Earl's Agent Orange been acting up, and Grandma split to go riding around the country with this bald trucker dude named Hairy. You don't ever want to tell the school your business, you're just asking for trouble.

"It's not what you think, Mr. Bowan," sez new teacher. "What's his name—Artie?—helped me break it up."

Mr. Bowan makes his neck grow long and jerks it to the right. "That true, R.D.? You wanted to break it up?"

I shrug, staring straight at him. Bowan just goes nuts when you look him in the eye and don't say nothing.

"I haven't got time for this, R.D. Why did you get involved?"

I nod toward the girl and sez, "We're blood." I don't know why I said it, but lately my voice is so deep, running so cool out of my mouth, I can't help using it to say bad-ass stuff.

"They're related?" asks new teacher. She's as brown as me with rad short black hair jelled up in all different directions and brown eyes wide with trying to figure things out.

"It means they're in the same gang," sez Bowan.

The girl lifts her face out of her hands. Goop is running from her eyes down her face in little black rivers. "I'm not no gangbanger."

Bowan looks her over good—hair ribbons, belt,

shoelaces, all okay—then lunges for the trash. He stretches the red rubber band thingie between his thumb and forefinger like he's going to shoot it at me. "I never figured you to be this dumb, R.D. You know gangs ain't—aren't—something to be fooling with."

I grin at his mistake. Bowan knows good English, but he sometimes forgets who college taught him to be, and goes back to being who he was raised. Even if he is Assistant Principal of Discipline at Buzz Aldrin Middle School in Goldhurst, California, smack in the middle of the San Joaquin Valley, he once told me he comes from a rough part of L.A. called Compton. "Just messin with ya, Mr. Bowan. I never joined no gang."

A whole lotta white shows under his eyeballs, bulging like brown peanut M&Ms. "Still, you know the consequences for fighting, R.D. You're suspended."

"What?" sez new teacher. "Mr. Bowan, if it weren't for Artie here . . ." Her hand falls onto my shoulder. She's so new she don't even know teachers aren't supposed to touch students. ". . . this little girl could have been seriously injured."

"School rules are school rules, Ms. Trueblood. If a student is involved in a fight, whether he started it or not, it's cause for suspension. R.D. knows this. If he wanted to help so bad he could have gone for another adult."

She flings her arms out from the elbows. "He's a hero in this."

Bowan stretches his neck like a turtle looking out his door. "That true, R.D.? You a he-ro?"

"Hell no, I just like to fight girls."

He gets all tense at the word "hell," even though it ain't much of a cussword.

The bell rings.

"Mr. Bowan," new teacher starts up, but he cuts her off. "Your first period is waiting for you, Ms. Trueblood."

She presses her lips closed and limps out the door.

Mr. Bowan sez, "Let's make it three days, R.D."

I try not to laugh. Three days off, laying around the house. I'm really getting punished now.

Miz Donaldson the principal swishes into the room, holding the daily bulletin she's about to read over the PA. She's always in a big hurry. She runs marathons, runs her own four kids around town, and runs Buzz Middle. I guess she likes running. "So that was you, R.D., in the fight? The first day of school—is that a record?"

"I guess, Miz Donaldson."

"Well, better ask your teachers what you missed when you get back. We don't want to have to give you your own parking space here." She and Bowan yuk it up.

It's the same old joke, that I'll be here so long I'll be driving myself to middle school. It used to make me mad till I found out middle schoolers have to move on when they turn sixteen—it's the law. I turn sixteen next Fourth of July. Last year I sort of tried at the beginning, thinking high school had to be better than this, but sure enough, I fell behind after my first couple of suspensions and never caught up. This year I can fart around all I want, get straight Fs, and they'll still have to send me to the high school cuz of social promotion.

I tuck my hands behind my head, knock my chair back on two legs, and rest against the wall. Yep, it's gonna be one kickback year. What's the use coming back on Thursday? Might as well take the rest of the week off.

# tЯee

EARL DIDN'T ANSWER Mr. Bowan's call though I knew he was home. I could picture him, his chicken legs sticking out from under the car he was changing the oil on, listening to the rings and cussing each one. Earl don't like to get the phone when he's in the middle of something, even if the call might mean more work. Our answering machine been broke for months. He keeps saying he's going to get a new one, but I think he likes the broke one. He don't like the work to pile up cuz it stresses him out.

Anyways, Officer Mendez comes into Mr. Bowan's office to drive me home. She's the cop at Buzz Middle, all the middle schools and high schools got them. We're walking to her cruiser and she sort of bounces on each step cuz she's always happy. "Hey, R.D.," she sez in her real loud voice that echoes in the hallway, "the first day of school—is that a record?"

"Yup." I can't remember what-all I've been suspended for—fighting, shooting Nerds out of a hollow Bic pen, saggin-and-baggin, mouthing off to a teacher, tagging a desk, which I didn't do but Mr. Bowan didn't believe me. I don't do half the stuff I get busted for. Sometimes I'm just near trouble and the teacher won't go on till someone takes the blame, and everybody is looking at me, so I figure what the hell, I could use a few days off. Teachers don't like me. I figured that out the first time I started kindergarten. After a couple of weeks the teacher told Grandma to keep me home another year cuz I didn't know none of my letters or numbers, but really it was cuz the teacher wanted to get rid of me.

"How's Grandma?" asks Officer Mendez.

"Fine." It still hurts some—her dumping me and Earl for Hairy.

"Grandpa?"

"Alright."

"Yeah?" Officer Mendez tilts her head and looks up at me with her big root beer eyes. She packs a loaded pistol about half her size. I stare at it, so close to me I could touch it.

I don't know if anyone could get Officer Mendez's gun away from her. She never does nothing but hang around the yard at break and lunch. The worst kind of guys hang round her—gangbangers and kids that ditch and tag and do drugs. She's even arrested some of them and they get mad at her and call her nasty names behind her back, but then they stand around her some more.

Officer Mendez picks up alot. She knows whose parents beat them, what kids are having sex and if they already have babies at home. She knows who stays out all night gang-banging, who busted whose head with a baseball bat last Friday night, whose family lives in a car. I wouldn't hang around no cop, but Officer Mendez knows me pretty well. She's made home visits.

She even arrested me once. It was last spring and I was walking to class and Ronaldo come up the side of me and pulled the strap of my backpack off my shoulder. I put it back on and he pulled it off and I put it back on and he pulled it off and I yelled, "Lay off of me, you frickin fruit," and stabbed his arm with the pen I was holding. It was a red pen and it broke the skin so I got assault and sexual harassment cuz Ronaldo really is a fruit. Officer Mendez walked me out to the parking lot and cuffed me right in front of the whole school, the kids gawking through the chain link fence like a herd of dumb cows.

By the time I got in the back of the cruiser, my legs were shaking and I was crying. I was afraid to go to jail, even juvie, cuz I've heard what guys do to other guys there. Then Officer Mendez started talking to me about her five kids and how it hadn't been easy for her, getting beat up with the vacuum cleaner cord by her stepdad, and running away, but she found her way and I would too.

Juvie turned out to be nothing much. One gangbanger about half my size with gang signs across his knuckles asked me to join up. Another guy offered me crack—he told me he kept it up his butt. Ha! So that's why they call it crack. All this crap went on, and I was only there one night.

Today me and Officer Mendez get into her cruiser and she

drives off. Even with the windows rolled up I can smell cow piss. There's alotta cows in Tulare County where Goldhurst is. I live pretty far from school and ride the bus cuz our school district makes all kinds of kids go to each middle school, so not just the preps go to Buzz Middle, the fancy new one. I wish I could just go to Lincoln Memorial, the ghetto school down at the end of my street. It don't have no gym or computer lab and the buildings are old and jacked up, but I'd rather roll out of bed at 8:10 and skate to school than have to be on the bus by seven o'clock.

We stop at one red light and Officer Mendez catches my eye in the rearview mirror. "I was hoping you'd behave yourself this year, make my life easier." I don't say nothing back and a minute later she tries again. "What are your grandparents going to say about this?"

"Nothing," and that's the truth. Grandma is long gone and old Earl never says much. He isn't my real grandpa, not even a step-one cuz Grandma never married him. We moved in with him the summer before second grade and after a while Grandma just started going by Mrs. Mitchell. The next school year when she had to fill out all the forms again she changed my name to Mitchell too. She said the school would be asking less questions about us that way.

# FOUR

WHEN OFFICER MENDEZ turns down my street she slows way down. There's little kids playing in their mud yards, spilling out onto the street, and dogs and chickens roaming around, and pregnant Hmong women walking with their shuffling grandpas.

Grandma told me when she was growing up everyone knew all their neighbors, but I don't know nobody cept Dominic and Scraps. Earl knows Old Man Luna next door cuz Earl grew up in this house with his sister Nadine. Now she lives in Oregon and hates us.

There are two houses on our street that are empty with boarded-up windows. One yard is full of dried cornstalks and yellow tomato vines. Only Old Man Luna's house is kept up nice, with a green lawn and all kinds of those whirly things stuck in the flower beds—windmills, birds, flowers— and the walkway is painted black to match the wrought iron fence. All kinds of stuff is piled in some yards: broken toys, rusty shopping carts, a washing machine, and sofas. Earl's place is the junkiest with tires, engines, and other spare car parts, some covered in blue plastic tarps with weeds growing up through the holes.

When Earl came home from Nam he worked in different auto shops, but he kept on losing one job after another cuz he couldn't work with nobody. He just started fixing cars at home and he's been doing it ever since. He's really not supposed to be working at all cuz he's on disability, but he makes people pay cash so the government don't catch him. He sez he's got to keep busy or go crazy.

There's a yellow Chevy Malibu sitting in our driveway next to Earl's old black Ford pickup and a gray Toyota sedan in the garage. Earl rolls out from under the Toyota. He's a scrawny white guy in an orange jumpsuit. He wears a greasy baseball cap over his thinning gray hair that ducktails in the back. Earl lights up a cigarette and coughs, holding his sunkin chest. He trudges across the lawn like every bone in his body is about to snap. "Lo, Officer," he sez.

"Hello, Mr. Mitchell. We couldn't get a hold of you on the phone. I'm sorry to have to tell you R.D. has been suspended three days for fighting."

Earl squints at me. He has all kinds of wrinkles bursting out around his eyes like the way little kids draw the sun. His skin is all crusty and splotchy from the Agent Orange, and there's scars across his nose where the skin cancers have been cut off. I stare down the street, not really seeing nothing, just Earl's disappointed face like I was still looking at him.

"I'm releasing R.D. into your custody, Mr. Mitchell. We expect you to keep him home."

"I know the drill, Officer."

"Good-bye, R.D. We'll see you Thursday." She leans closer, her head coming up to about my shoulder. "Not Friday, not Monday, Thursday." She smiles at Earl and sez, "At this rate how is he ever going to make it to college? Right, Mr. Mitchell?"

Earl nods, though he's never been to college himself. The Marine recruiter hooked him right outside his own high school gym, using a shiny brochure about flying helicopters as bait. Earl figured he'd get drafted in the army anyways so he joined up. He couldn't pass some damn writing test though, so he ended up fixing copters instead of flying them, and doing a whole lot of other crap he never planned on.

After Officer Mendez drives off, Earl asks, "What was you fighting about?"

"I don't know."

He squints into my face. "You don't look messed up any. What's the other guy look like?"

It was two *girls,* I'm thinking, but I sez, "Kinda messed up."

He laughs, coughs, wheezes, sez, "Stay close to the house. You know I hate getting called down to the courthouse having to explain myself to that judge."

"I know."

"Chicken needs frying later on."

"I don't know how to fry chicken."

"You could learn."

"I like your cooking, Earl. Yours is the best."

"Well then, pair up the socks on the dryer. You know how to do that, don't you?" He's not real mad at me, I can tell. When he's just a little mad he orders me around, when he's real mad he won't say nothing. Grandma called it "the silent treatment." Then he sez, "I'll be in later. I've got to fix the timing on this Malibu."

"Can I drive it into the garage for you?"

"You don't have a driver's license."

"Come on, Earl. I'll stay on the driveway. I'll be real careful."

"Why should I let you drive when you can't even last one day at school?"

"Cuz it would be helping you."

He smiles then, those sunbursts exploding around his eyes. "Back the Toyota out of the garage instead, while I drive the Malibu in, then pull up behind." The Toyota ain't as good as the Malibu so it's kind of like a punishment.

I run to the Toyota and jump in. Crap, it's a stick. I'm not that good at driving sticks. I push the clutch in and slowly ease into reverse. I hunch my shoulders to my ears, afraid to hear even the tiniest sound of grinding gears. I give it a little gas, release the clutch, and slowly roll down the drive. Perfect. Earl pulls the Malibu in. I ease the clutch out, but start rolling too fast down the slope of the driveway. I panic, jam the stick into first with a screeching whine. Damn! I pull up, set the brake, and climb out. I hand the keys to Earl feeling like I really messed up, but he don't say nothing.

I go through the back door past the socks piled in the clothes basket, thinking I'll get to them later. In the kitchen I grab the loaf of bread and head to my room. I switch on my CD player and sit on the bed in the lumpy middle of twisted blankets, bobbing my head to the beat. I take out a slice of bread, fold it, jam it into my mouth in two bites, then take out another slice and another slice until the loaf is half gone.

I spend twenty minutes on my Xbox, getting to the level that's fun, then die in two seconds. I wish I could stop playing, but my finger pushes the start button without me really wanting it to. I remember I was looking forward to school starting cuz it's boring at home, but then school's boring too. I flop back on my bed and set my arm over my eyes.

Sometimes when I'm laying around I get to thinking about things I don't want to think about. I remember in the beginning of summer Grandma going out to the Palace Indian Gaming Center in Lemoore, where she was hanging out with Hairy. Me and Earl should have knowed something was up, the way she pranced on out of here in her red high heels and yellow-flower stretch pants. Grandma is younger than Earl, with long hair dyed black, high reddish-brown cheekbones, and brown eyes full of fun. The day she split with Hairy, she left phone numbers on the fridge—Hairy's trucking company's number and his home phone. He lives clear out in Kentucky or Tennessee or somewheres—I get all those faraway states mixed up. That night after dinner, when Earl lit up, he yanked the numbers off the fridge and set the match to them.

"Far out," he said, staring into the flame, and he never sez "far out." I guess he was pretty drunk. "This reminds me of draft card burning." He told me it was what guys did when they didn't want to go fight in Nam.

"Do you wish you never went to Nam, Earl?"

"I'm a damn fool, boy, and I'll tell you why. If I had it to do over again, I'd do it all the same damn way, the Vietnam War and your grandma too. That's a sad thing," said Earl. "That's a real sad thing."

# five

I WAKE UP TO the smell of chicken frying—yum, my favorite. I'm sure hungry. I stretch my legs and feel something next to my feet, my pile of paired socks. Good old Earl! He only asks once and then he does things himself. He hates nagging worse than anything, which makes things pretty quiet around here since Grandma left. I go into the living room and turn on the TV just to make some noise in the house besides Earl's coughing. It's got a lot worse since Grandma left, like he held in as many coughs as he could when she was around, and now he feels he can let them all out.

At first when Grandma said she was leaving, I was real angry at her and started yelling I didn't want to move. When she got me to understanding it was just her going, I got kind of excited to see her go. She was the one making me go to school and do chores. With just old Earl I knew I could do pretty much what I wanted.

Then she got all guilty and started talking about her lousy life, how she was forced to get married too young to a guy she didn't love and live with in-laws who didn't want her around. She's got a big family out in Dinuba, but when she got pregnant in her senior year, they kicked her out of the house. But you can't keep Grandma down. She went to beauty school and did hair and quietly saved her money. When my real grandpa started chasing other women, she moved out with Yolanda, who was just a toddler then. Grandma told me she'd been unlucky in love. Hairy was the real thing and her chance to have some fun.

"You used to have fun with Earl," I reminded her.

When Grandma first met Earl in a bar, he had on his Goldhurst Harley-Davidson club jacket. Before long Grandma had her own leathers. They were black with fringe down the arms and legs, and the pants were the kind you wear over other pants cuz the back is cut out of them. Every time she turned around, I'd forget her bubble butt was dressed in jeans and sticking out of black leather fringe and I just had to cover my eyes, but Grandma was proud as hell of that outfit. She and Earl would go on trips with a bunch of other old people in their Harley club. She had me going to three churches and every church had youth group overnight trips and summer camps. She'd send me to those church things so she and Earl could take off on his Harley. After a while they went less and less, and then one day the Harley had a For Sale sign on it.

When I reminded Grandma of the Harley, she said, "Yeah, well Earl got old fast," and then she asked did I think she was a terrible person, and I said no. She said, "I wouldn't be going if it meant leaving Earl alone. Earl wouldn't know what to do without you."

Earl calls me to dinner and there's broccoli with the chicken and baked potato. We always have potatoes or bread, but no rice ever. Earl sez he won't eat no Gook food, not after Nam, but he does a good job on spaghetti or chuck roast and sometimes he even makes waffles for dinner. After Grandma left I realized Earl has always done most of the cooking and cleaning. I tried to think what Grandma did, besides hold Tupperware parties, watch "Jerry! Jerry! Jerry!" and go to the Palace. I know she added something around here that's missing now. Earl used to say Grandma's laugh sounded like a bull moose, but he smiled when he said it. When we used to watch football, Grandma would spring off the sofa shouting, "Oh, hell no!" when the Raiders fumbled, and Earl would laugh till his wheezing wouldn't let him laugh no more.

When Grandma first left she called every day, then about once a week, then she quit calling so much. She used to leave messages that went, "Earl, are you there, are you there? Dammit, Earl, pick up." Maybe that's why Earl likes the answering machine broke. Sometimes I miss Grandma, but she would rather be with Hairy instead of us, so let her.

We eat, and after Earl washes the dishes, we watch *Jeopardy*. I hate *Jeopardy* but Earl likes it, and it's comfortable sunk into the old brown sofa, Earl with his beer, me with my Mountain Dew, the big bag of peanuts between us. Earl lights up and coughs. He holds his chest and wheezes.

Grandma tried to get him to quit, but he sez it's his goddamn American right to smoke, it's the Agent Orange that wrecked his lungs, not smoking. He catches a breath, then takes another puff. He coughs, he wheezes, then he's quiet. When the sofa starts to shake I realize he's been too quiet too long. His eyes are bugged out, the splotches on his face are flaming purple.

"Earl! Earl! You okay?" I pound him on the back and his head reels forward, his cigarette dropping out of his hand. I jump up and stomp on it, forgetting I have bare feet, but it's like I don't even feel the burn. Earl flops to his side. I sit him up again and shake him. I want to call 911, but another time when I did, Earl got done with his coughing spell in time to answer the door and say no one needs an ambulance here. Then he cussed me out and told me to never call no ambulance cuz they cost an arm and a leg.

I tear through the house looking for his inhaler. He's got a bunch of them, and when the inhalers are empty he don't throw them out. I gather them off the kitchen counter, the coffee table, the bathroom, and toss them in his lap. He shakes his head no, points to his room. I run in there and dig in his dirty overalls back pocket and find the inhaler he's using now. I run to him, press it to his mouth. He takes a weak hit, then another stronger one, he shudders, he wheezes, then thank Jesus, he's breathing again.

He croaks, "Get me up." Spit is dripping down the front of his shirt, and it's really gross with yellow mucus and flecks of blood in it, but that ain't nothing new.

I grab him under his arms and I pull him to his feet, and

it's like lifting up a scarecrow. He staggers down the hall. I want to follow him to make sure he's going to be okay, but I know I can't. It's like Grandma told me long time ago, we got to pretend nothing's wrong with him, it's the only way Earl can stand being as sick as he is. I hear water running in his bathroom sink. There's more coughs. A hanger whacks against the closet ceiling, and I know he's getting a clean shirt.

I tiptoe back to the sofa and pretend to be real interested in *Jeopardy* when Earl, okay this time, sits back down.

## Six

LATER we hear the rumbling muffler of Bobby Scudder's Pontiac in the drive. Bobby's a real loser, I can't stand him. He still lives at home with his mom, and I swear all she feeds him is salami sandwiches. He owns his own "business," about a half dozen vending machines, dropped off at the bowling alley and bars, so old and cheap people keep losing their money in them and tipping them over. Bobby and Earl went to high school together and they both went to Nam, but at different places. Anyways, I'm glad someone else is here, even if it is Bobby.

I open the door, and Bobby sez, "Hey worthless, you still live here?" When he laughs his tongue sticks out between yellow snaggle teeth. He's got a bulging gut he can't button his shirt over. He's carrying a twelve-pack.

Earl doesn't get drunk every night, but with Bobby around, he's sure to. Bobby is a loud, mean drunk who talks dirty about women and will take a swing at any guy who won't swing back. Earl is a sad drunk who just gets quieter and sadder until he passes out. Grandma is a happy drunk, and she used to say Earl and her were good drinking buddies cuz they evened each other out.

Bobby is wearing his greasy old "Vietnam Veteran" cap. He's always talking about Nam, making himself out to be a war hero. Probably it's a big deal to him cuz it was the only time he left his mommy. Earl never talks about the war.

I step out on the porch and shout back, "I'm going out in front."

"Stay close to the house," Earl hollers back.

I can hear the slap of Scraps's skateboard, going off the ramp he's made for himself on the street. There's a clink, then silence as he sails over a shopping cart, then the solid slam of his landing. Scraps skates 24/7, lives it, dreams it. I skate, but my board is broke, and I don't have the money to fix it. I suck at stunts, and don't try nothing too hard, but Scraps is a crazy man. Once he skated off the school roof and got his ankle broke, but he didn't care. He said it was worth it.

"Hey R.D., lucky, you got outta school."

"Hey."

We slap palms, clamp curled fingers, and knock fists. Scraps is a little skinny guy with freckles all over his body. He has light brown hair that hangs straight down to his chin. About the only part of his face you can see is his long thin needle nose. "What you been doing all day?"

"Just chillin."

"I heard Earl coughing clear out here. My mom sez he better quit smoking."

"It ain't the cigarettes, it's the Agent Orange."

"Who's that?"

"Not who—what. It's this liquid fire stuff they poured on the trees in Nam to burn off the leaves so they could see the enemy. The copters would come back to base with it all stuck on the tail and they never thought to clean it off. Earl would slide under a copter to work on it and he breathed it in. It burned his skin, too."

"That's messed up."

"Tell me. What's up at school?"

"I caught up with you guys." All these years Scraps been one grade behind me and Dominic. Now that he's caught up, he won't let us forget it. He moves the shopping cart a little to the left, it rolls some, he fixes it some more. He flips his hair out of his face and sez, "We're in the same core. Dominic, too. We've got this new teacher. They dumped all the dumb kids on her."

"Can't be all of them—there's too many." Out of the four hundred or so eighth graders last year, eighty-six flunked. I know cuz one day when I got sent to Mr. Bowan's office he wasn't there, but the retention list was sitting right on his desk so I snuck a peek. It takes three semester Fs to flunk. You can go to summer school to make some up. Summer school is super easy, like the only thing you gotta do is show up. I went for something like two days, but it was boring and too early so I just slept in and forgot about it.

"There's some smart kids in our class too," sez Scraps. "Mostly new kids. Teacher said she just got hired three days ago. They had to make another class last minute. She made us go around the room and introduce ourselves."

"Oh crap, not that kinda teacher."

"And we have to do projects, build castles and stuff. She sez she wants us to relive history."

"I'm not doing no projects. They got to send me up to high school next year no matter what."

"It don't matter to me if I ever get to high school," sez Scraps. I know what's coming next, I heard it a hundred times. "I'm gonna be a pro skater and get sponsored. I'm gonna live in Long Beach."

*Screech-screech.* It's too dark to see Dominic coming cuz we got no street lights, but we can hear him scraping the length of every car he passes with a bottle cap or piece of metal, whatever he found in the street. Earl don't let him in our house no more cuz he likes to mess things up. Like when we snuck into the house with the Keep Out sign. I was happy to just sit around the candle we brought, chillin, but Dominic had to singe Southside gang signs in the carpet.

He comes into our porch light. He's kinda medium built, and he walks with his knees turned out cuz he's saggin-and-baggin so much his pants will fall to his ankles if he don't. He's wearing a blue bandanna, which could get him hurt in this neighborhood. Crazy homie, claiming blue and living on the Northside.

I hold my palm up to him, but he charges me and socks my shoulder so hard I gotta take a step back to keep from falling down. Man, it hurts. I wanna rub it, but I'm not giving him the satisfaction. "What the—?"

"I heard you was defending red."

25

It takes me a minute to remember back to the cat fight. "You're trippin, dude. Where'd you get your info?"

"Officer Mendez, foo, and she don't lie. She asked me about you."

"What'd you tell her?"

"I don't say nothing to no cop."

If Dominic didn't look ready to kill me, I'd laugh. He brags to Officer Mendez 24/7. Mostly it's about his uncle Jaime, who just got out of prison and is the reason Dominic claims blue. He calls Dominic BB—baby banger—and keeps saying he's gonna take him out gangbanging. So every Saturday night Dominic gets all dressed in blue and hides his mama's kitchen knife down his pants and waits and waits for his uncle to come by. Dominic never sez nothing about it on Sunday mornings but you can tell by the beat dog look in his eyes, his uncle never showed.

I sez, "You know I don't got a color. I was up too close to the cat fight and this fat mama kicked me so I kicked her back, right in the ass."

"She pegged our core teacher a good one. She was limping all day," sez Scraps.

"Who you talking to, White Boy?" Dominic's been calling Scraps White Boy all summer. I never seen him any different from us. Sure, me and Dominic ditch him sometimes cuz he gets on our nerves. His mom don't let him do all the stuff we can, like running around late at night. Still, we all grew up together on this same street so I figure we're all homies.

Scraps pretends like things are cool with Dominic. He

rolls toward his ramp while Dominic watches him. Scraps launches off his ramp. Him sailing through the air is a thing to watch, every muscle in his body sez he's going to land it.

Dominic sticks out his foot and shoves the shopping cart a few inches forward so Scraps' back wheels catch the wire edge. He lands on his feet and one hand, but the grocery cart crashes down on his back.

Dominic laughs. For about one minute, he's happy.

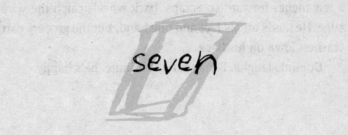

# seven

THURSDAY MORNING, cold and gray. I step out of Bus 34 rubbing my arms. *Brr!* It could rain. Our bus is the first to get to Buzz Middle, fifty minutes before the first bell. Buzz is decorated with old-fashioned space stuff, like there's a model of a space capsule in front next to the loading zone that's always getting tagged. Even the wastebaskets in the yard are shaped like little rockets. All of this is pretty lame seeing how everyone knows the moon landing was a fake. The doors of the Neil Armstrong Auditorium are shut, but I can still hear the jazz band screeching away.

Band—now there's something I don't get. Yeah right, in fifth grade I wanted to play an instrument like all the other kids. But Grandma said no, it costs too much. I told her the school would lend me an instrument, but she said there was all kinds of extras like special shoes to march in and these things called reeds. The school said they'd get that stuff for the kids that couldn't pay, but Grandma just shook her head and said, "We don't want to be in with that bunch." Now I think she just didn't want to be bothered yelling at me to practice and listening to those sick cow sounds beginners make. I'm glad I didn't get into it. Think about it—smashing a hard metal thing against your mouth and blowing into it. It can't feel good. And what comes out is not rock or rap or anything cool, but old people's music. Buzz Middle's marching band even has Star Trekkie uniforms with weird pointy things sticking out of their shoulders like wings. And the band kids always have to fund raise cuz they take trips, once all the way to Disney World. But man, it was just too much cookie dough to sell, so all the kids I know couldn't make it, just the rich kids whose parents can write out a check.

A cold wind rises up and whacks the back of my head. I wish I wore my flannel overshirt, but it looks so cool running around in just a plain white T-shirt, like you can take it.

Scraps and Dominic and them others on Bus 34 head toward the cafeteria. I hardly ever get breakfast cuz standing in that line tells the whole school you're free-and-reduced. Lunch line isn't the same cuz when you hand over your lunch card no one knows how much you paid for it, but free-and-reduced can't use it on the fast food carts—you gotta eat cafeteria slop.

The air smells like those French toast sticks that are pretty good with the little containers of maple syrup you dip into. The line is starting to move so I just sort of walk back and forth thinking I'll duck in at the last moment with nobody noticing.

Just then the auditorium doors fly open and I'm face to

face with a honey-blonde girl I've never seen before. I look straight into her wide green eyes but she's gone somewhere in her thoughts. She's not dressed like a middle schooler, but more like the kind of college kid you see in movies. She's like standing in a cloud, her sweater is so white and fluffy with one pale blue snowflake in the middle. Her cherry lips are puffy, like she's been kissing, kissing half the night, and I can't help staring at them.

There's streams of kids passing on both sides of her. I step to my right, she steps to her left. I step to my left, she steps to her right. I like dancing this crazy kind of dance with this pretty girl, so I step to my right again. She sez, "Excuse me," in a soft, husky voice, then darts around me with a little skip.

She makes a sharp turn around the corner. I wait a few seconds, then follow her around the building to watch her cross the basketball courts. She's got one of those expensive haircuts that curls over her shoulders. Her short preppy skirt swings with the movement of her hips. She's lugging a big long instrument case, not like the little flutes most girls play. I wonder what's inside it. I don't know all the instruments' names. It's probably why her lips are so red and bunchy, been pressed against that big cold metal thing. She has it all, but still she has to pick the biggest, dumbest band instrument she can find.

I pick up a rock, aim, and throw it after her. It thuds against the case and bounces off. She stops, slowly turns, and I duck around the building. There's a heavy lump in my gut and I'm not hungry anymore.

I start walking across the yard toward my homies' table.

I'm jerked backward and yanked to the side. Someone's got hold of the straps of my backpack and is swinging me around. Next thing I know the dude is in front of me, grabbing me by the shoulders.

It's not a dude, it's a *girl.*

"Hey, homie!" She's little but she's got a real loud voice. Her big smile looks extra white against her brown skin. Her eyebrows are shaved off and drawn back on in black pencil, shaped like horseshoes so she looks real surprised. She also drew a black line around her lips and filled it in with kind of a red mud color. Her bangs are jelled into two strings dangling before her eyes. Her body lotion smells spicy, like cookies warm from the oven. It takes me a sec to figure out who she is cuz she was so messed up the last time I seen her. Now all she's got is three skinny lines of scab down the side of her face from the cat fight. "I been looking for your ass, R.D."

"Who told you my name?"

"Someone. I'm Desiree." We slap palms, grab curled fingers, and knock fists. "I went to Merit Reform last year."

"What for?"

"For fighting."

"Fo sure? I thought you was a beginner."

"Shut up. That biatch weighed a ton." She throws her shoulders back and sticks her titties out and sort of gives them a shake at me.

"Is it true at Merit you only gotta go till two?"

"Yep. And hardly do no work, except for the guys. They got that boot camp stuff and some guys just puke all day. Did you get into trouble with your grandparents?"

I look at her hard cuz for sure she's been asking around about me. Her eyes flash and dart. They're a real pretty color, like fudge candy. "Earl don't care what I do."

"I thought my sister was gonna whoop me, but when I told her that fat biatch jumped me for no reason she got all sweet."

"You tell her you're claiming red?"

"Not no more! It was my first day, you know? This one girl comes up to me and sez I could have all kinds of cool friends to hang with, so I sez okay. She gives me that red thingie to put in my hair and the next thing—*bam*—I'm flat on the cement. I didn't tell none of that to Luz. If I mess up she'll send me back to our mom, and me and her boyfriend don't get along. Don't you got a mom?"

I shrug. I don't usually say nothing about my mom, but this Desiree is real easy to talk to. "She's in Chino."

"You mean like the prison? That all-women's facility they got down there?" Desiree's eyes snap wide. "Oh! Did she shoot your daddy?"

"Naw, she's a crackhead. Got busted for dealing."

"You miss her?"

I shrug. "It's hard to remember her." I was only about four when Grandma kicked Yolanda out for good. She was more like a big sister to me than a mom anyways. Grandma had to raise us both at the same time. Yolanda used to get down on the floor and play GI Joes with me. I hated playing GI Joes, but I liked having someone to play with.

"Hey, wanna hang out at lunch? I got money. I can get us something good."

I don't have no money, and I don't want to eat no cafeteria slop, so she's got me interested. "I'll try to make it, if I don't get busy."

"Ow!" She swings and socks me hard in the arm. She's wearing the same tight black stretchy top and the same black bra with the tiny red rosebud. She catches me looking down there so I sez, "It looks like you're still claiming red."

She grins and looks up at me a little cross-eyed between the dangling ropes of hair. "Are you going out?"

"Naw." I ain't asked a girl out since seventh grade—what's the use? You got to be with that girl at lunch with all her friends giggling, and you got nothing to say to her. I'd rather be hangin with my homies.

The bell rings.

"Oh, crap, I got PE first," sez Desiree. "I'm gonna ask coach if I don't have to dress out cuz I'm on my period."

I hate hearing about that, but girls are always talking about it like it's nothing.

"Meet me at the green umbrella cart." She walks off real slow, her little butt wagging.

Hell, she's trouble for sure, but she's got things stirred up inside me.

eight

CORE CLASS—it's like half your life, three periods—English, literature, history. Walking in there, I see all the kids getting out their stuff, picking up right where they left off, and I don't know what they're doing. The thing about being suspended is that school goes on without you. No matter how many times I've been suspended, this always catches me by surprise. Dominic is sitting right here in the last seat in the first row, closest to the door. I slap palms, grasp curled fingers, and knock fists with him, then ask where I sit. He nods toward the last seat, fifth row.

Like Scraps told me, the teacher is the new one from the fight. She's got "Ms. Trueblood" written in neat cursive on the board. She's all busy going around the room, still limping some. The kid next to me is waving his whole arm like crazy, calling, "Teacher, teacher, teacher" in a flat tone. He's got two yellow buck teeth and a flaming pizza face. When Miz Trueblood gets to him, he sez, "I need a pencil."

"Selwyn! What happened to the pencil I gave you yesterday?"

"I had it in my backpack, I did, but the boys I live with took it."

Not brothers, but boys he lives with, meaning a group home. Once the juvie judge got mad at Grandma and Earl and said if they couldn't keep me home during my suspensions he was going to make me a ward of the county and have CPS—Child Protection Services—put me in a group home. I'd rather go to jail.

Miz Trueblood hands Selwyn a pencil then turns to me. "Oh, R.D., welcome to class."

"Did I miss anything?"

That question just kills teachers. "In three days! You've missed a lot. We got started on our coat of arms, and most students will be finishing up today." She starts explaining about heraldry, how noblemen in the Middle Ages designed their shields to show who they were. Oh God, the Middle Ages, the exact same thing we did last year. Repeating really is repeating! She hands me a piece of paper with a blank shield drawn on it. She tells me to draw a symbol representing myself in each of the four sections.

"I don't get it."

"Well, have you ever played on a team?"

"No."

"Do you play a musical instrument?"

"No."

"Do you belong to a certain church?"

"No."

"Do you skateboard?"

"No." By now I'm just playing with her.

"Think, R.D. What have been your accomplishments in life?"

"Nothing. Can I just draw four zeros?"

She starts to move away from my desk, her voice so cold, it's like coming out of the freezer. "If that's what you think of yourself, go ahead."

I take my pencil and draw four fat zeros, one in each section. I shove my paper aside, stretch my feet out into the aisle, and cross my arms over my mighty chest. I look around and notice the kids are mostly repeaters like me. Then I spot her—that pretty prep girl in the sweater cloud. Her green eyes get wide, then squint, then cut away from me. It surprises me cuz she seemed kind of sweet this morning. I didn't make her out to be stuck up.

Miz Trueblood is suddenly at my desk. "R.D., why aren't you working?"

"I'm done." I hand it to her.

She looks it over with a tight look on her face and hands it back. "Put your name on the back."

I turn the paper over and put R.D. with the R inside the D—my trademark.

"Your complete first and last name, please. In cursive."

"I don't know cursive."

"Write your name," she sez too loud. It happens that way to me all the time. Teachers try to stay calm and then they lose it so suddenly it even surprises them.

I look around some more. Scraps is busy gluing his fingers together, then spreading them out real slow, enjoying that tugging feel on his skin. Dominic is hunched over his work, shading a part in with the side of his pencil, looking "on task" as teachers say, but he's also got his hand down next to his desk, using scissors to gouge chunks of that corky bulletin board stuff out of the wall. When he gets a handful of cork, he launches it with his ruler at the back of Scraps' neck. Some of it goes down his shirt, but even better, some of it hits the girl next to him.

She squeals, "Someone's throwing stuff. It got in my hair."

Miz Trueblood goes over and picks the cork stuff out of the girl's hair. "What is it?"

"The wall," sez another girl.

"The wall! Which direction did it come from?"

No one sez anything, but enough eyes turn toward Dominic that Miz Trueblood looks at him too. "Dominic, did you throw this?"

"No." He continues his work. The scissors are nowhere in sight.

Miz Trueblood walks over to him and inspects the wall. It takes her a while to look under his desk. "Dominic! I'm going to have to send you to Mr. Bowan."

"I didn't do it. It was like that when I got here."

"But you were throwing it."

"I know you'd never believe me cuz I'm Mexican."

"Oh no, that's not going to work with me. Take a look." She's pointing at her own face which is as brown as his, and all the kids laugh at new teacher taking on Dominic. She nods toward an empty desk at the end of the third row and sez, "Sit there for now."

The excitement is over, at least for now. Most of the kids go back to work on their coat of arms. The girls are drawing double hearts to mean friendship and crosses to show they're Christians and music notes cuz they're in band. The guys make footballs and skateboards and some of them do crosses and notes too. Here they've been working for a couple of days and I'm already done. This class is easy.

Miz Trueblood comes up to me again and sez, "While you're waiting, R.D., I can check your literature book out to you. It's a brand new book and it's to remain in good condition. If you write any graffiti in it or lose it, you'll have to pay for it and it's sixty-two dollars. Read something in it now. Don't waste your time sitting around."

It cracks me up when teachers say that. Hell, time is all I got, hours and hours of it at school and at home, and it's all boring.

I open the book, but I don't really read it, just look at the pictures.

I find a painting of a big city in pink and dark blue. There's an old black man too. A few words in big lettering is the old guy talking about his razor. The best thing about core is sometimes the teacher will put on a CD of a guy reading one of the stories. We have to use the CD cuz most kids can't read good. We're supposed to follow along, but I just pretend, and then when I hear turning pages, I turn too. I wish we could hear this story right now, but Miz Trueblood sez, "It's time to form groups to discuss your Middle Ages projects. Choose a subject and assign a job to each group member."

Dominic and Scraps come running over to me. We slap hands and curl fingers and knock knuckles. Then we get real still and stare at each other. If we're all together, who's gonna do the work?

Dominic points to three preps. "They're the smart kids. Let's get with them."

As soon as we go over there Miz Trueblood sez, "This is too many." She points in one direction. "Dominic, you go into that group." She directs Scraps to the opposite corner. "Gilbert, you go there."

It would be okay to sit with the preps if I had Dominic and Scraps with me, but by myself it's a little scary. I pull up a chair and sit across from the pretty band girl. She looks straight at me and crinkles her green eyes, then looks away. She like already hates me, and I didn't do nothing.

"Weren't you in eighth grade last year?" sez the girl next to me.

I don't say nothing back, just dog her. She's Yesenia, one of the Arcadio kids. They're like famous cuz their dad owns three car junkyards in the valley—Arcadio Auto Recyclers—and the whole family is on TV in commercials. Junk car parts must be good money cuz they're rich. Their house is like a mansion. It's got a swimming pool, tennis courts, everything. I been there cuz when I was in kindergarten Yeni's brother Miguel invited the whole class to his birthday party. Grandma bought me a Nerf ball to give him, and then when I got to the party I seen that they were giving Nerf balls for party favors so I chucked my gift in the bushes.

"Let's build a castle," Yeni sez, real bossy. "I can buy the stuff. Sugar cubes work best, and I can get little flags and knights and stuff from this cake decorating store I know. What do you want to do, Jeanette?"

Jeanette—so that's the name of the pretty band girl. Jeanette is not a kid's name. The only other Jeanette I ever heard of is a friend of my grandma. "I like to write," she sez. "I'll do the report. Do you want to design the castle, Sterling?"

Sterling, like sterling silver, like his parents thought he was better than everyone else the day he was born. He's a beefy kid with bleached hair and dark roots, an expensive dye job. Jeanette blinks at him and tilts her head. He nods his big chin back at her, his eyes half-closed like he's sleepy. Already they got something going on.

"What do I do?" I ask.

"Nothing," sez Yeni, "you just get an A. You're just lucky you're with us. I gotta get As on everything cuz I'm going to UCLA." She gives her little stretchy shirt a tug, like it really can cover the roll of brown bread dough oozing out of her low riders.

"I want to do something," I sez. I don't know why but I do.

"He can find pictures of castles to base our model on," sez Jeanette, not looking at me. "We can meet at my house on Sunday to do the construction. How about one o'clock?"

Silver Boy nods. "Cool. I'll be there." He's got a brand new snowboarding jacket slung on the back of his chair with all kinds of zippers and straps. I wonder what snowboarding is like.

Jeanette sez her address and we all write it down just as the bell rings.

Miz Trueblood is too new to tell us to pack up two minutes before. Everyone rushes out, leaving stuff scattered all over. The only two kids left are me and the group home kid. He's trying to shove his literature book into his cheap backpack.

Miz Trueblood runs over and pulls it out. "You don't have to take home your book unless we have an assignment in it." She like knows she'll never see her new sixty-two-dollar book if the group home gets a hold of it. She places it back in his desk.

He looks at her, trudges to the door, slowly turns to look back, and sez, "Bye, Miz Trueblood. Love you."

She opens her mouth, but can't think of nothing to say to that. When he disappears, she looks around the room and sighs. I'm not a school boy or nothing, but I pick up a few colored pencils and hand them to her.

"Thank you, R.D. Would you like to discuss your missed work now?"

"I don't have time. I got first lunch."

"How about after school?"

I notice Sterling's jacket left behind and pick it up like it's mine. "I gotta catch the bus."

She sighs again and picks up some scraps of paper. At the door, I reach into Dominic's desk and slip out his literature book. I don't know why.

# nine

I HEAD TOWARD the green umbrella. Just then someone jumps me from behind, yanking my backpack. It's just Desiree, but already this is getting old.

"Hey, I been waiting for ya, R.D. Let's go."

We stand in the fast food cart line when two girls with horseshoe eyebrows and black rings around their lips same as Desiree come screaming up to her. They start pulling her toward the girls' bathroom.

"Hey, stop," she yells at them. She's a powerful yeller.

"We gotta tell ya something," one of them sez.

"Tell me later."

"Come on, Desi," sez the other one, "don't you gotta change your pad?" They both scream and giggle.

"Hey! I don't wear no pad!" Desiree yells, and I wanna cover my ears.

After more pulling and pleading, Desiree sez she'll go with them.

The line is moving slow, but we're so close to the cart that if she leaves now, we'll lose our spot. She holds out two dollar bills, rolled up like cigarettes, one in each hand. "Get us two fries, and I'll meet you at the tables."

My hands move out to grab the money, but somehow they go past it and land on Desiree's boobs, and I give them a quick squeeze. God, I've never done that before. I even surprised myself, out in the middle of the school yard, right in front of everybody. The way she shakes them right in your face you know she wants you to. I take the money.

Desiree's looking at me goofy-like. "Do you want to go out?"

I'm kind of dazed, touching boobs, getting money, and drooling over fries all at once so I'm not sure what happens next.

I must've nodded, cuz she sez "cool," and is off like a bullet.

Wait a minute! Crap! Does she think we're going out?

I don't have much time to think about it. Next thing I know it's my turn at the cart and then I'm holding two loads of delicious fries, a squiggle of red ketchup on top of each one. I'm walking toward the tables, and then a funny thing happens. I just keep walking, past the edge of the courtyard, past the basketball courts, across the football field, all the way to the baseball diamond. I twist around to see if any teachers are after me, and then when I see the coast is clear I duck behind the backstop. There ain't no kids back there hooked up or smoking. There's no one to see me step into the bushes and slip through a hole in the chain link fence.

On the other side is the park. I walk across it and down a

little hill, and crawl into a big old drain pipe. I start to eat the fries, which are still warm after all that way. I get out the literature book and flip it open. A blob of ketchup falls on it and I smear it clear across the page. It's not Dominic's book no more, it's not the school's, it's mine now, I made my mark.

The rain starts to patter as soft as cat feet. I pull Silver Boy's jacket out of my backpack and put it over me like a blanket. It's warm and cozy. I find the page with the old black homeless man, look over all the pictures, and read all the big print. Usually that's enough for me, but this story looks cool, with gangbangers and everything. I read it all. At the end I turn the page and I'm surprised it's over. It makes me stop and think. I don't get it. The gangbangers got scared away too easy. Still I liked the old guy's name—Lemon Brown—and the cool way he talked about singing the blues and cutting a week into nine days with his razor. It was a pretty good story. I shut the book, snuggle down into the jacket and listen to the rain. This is fine, I think. This is living.

# ten

I MUST'VE DOZED OFF. It's getting dark. The rain has stopped, but it's real cold. I've missed the bus, even the late one, and I'm miles from home. I don't even have change to call Earl.

I walk a few blocks until I get on a road with a City Coach stop. I have to beg money. Me and Dominic did this once to make money, telling people we needed bus fare to get home. We got a few bucks. But the sad thing is now I need bus fare for reals. It takes me four tries.

The bus ride is about an hour to my neighborhood with all the stops and one transfer, and then it's about a quarter-mile walk down my street. By then, it's past eight. Earl won't yell at me, he never yells at me, but I might have worried him. It's hard to tell what Earl is thinking cuz he never sez.

I climb the porch steps, wondering if he's started to drink yet. The light is on in the living room and the TV's on, but Earl's nowhere in sight. There's a pie slice of light coming from the bathroom which explains things.

I could sneak into my room and say I been there the whole time and fell asleep. Earl might buy it if he's drunk enough. The trick is to get past the bathroom without him seeing me. I take one giant step, my eyes sliding toward the bathroom door, hoping I won't see old Earl on the can and have him see me seeing him.

He's not on the can. He's curled up on the floor, his jeans down around his ankles, his eyes wide, and his gray tongue sticking out. His body lets out one mournful fart, his digestive juices settling down for good, his sorry old body singing its sad good-bye song.

# eLeven

I JUST KEEP WALKING, right down the hall. I go to my room, throw off my backpack and the big snowboard jacket that's making me sweat now. My mind is saying here's my room just the way I left it this morning, nothing's changed. Here's my bed with the blankets all twisted up in a heap, here's my clothes thrown all over the floor, my CD player, my Xbox, my skateboard with the trashed trucks, my life, same as always. Nothing's changed, except Earl is dead so everything's changed.

I should feel really bad about him, but all I can think is what's gonna happen to me. I thought my life was messed up before.

CPS will put me in a home. Maybe I'll be in the same home with Selwyn and he'll try to be my friend. The best I can hope for is a foster home where people just take in foster kids to make some money and you have to watch them spend it on their own kids while you get hand-me-downs. I can't believe Earl's dead. I know I gotta go back there and have another look. It just takes me a minute to get up the nerve.

I take another peek. He's dead alright.

If only I didn't ditch, if I went home on the bus like I was supposed to, I would've been here when he went down. Oh, Earl, sorry, sorry.

I go into the living room to sit down, but I can't sit down. I just walk around and around, wearing a hole in the carpet, Grandma used to say. Grandma. I need to call her, but Earl burned up all her numbers. I need to call someone, but who? Maybe one of the neighbors, Old Man Luna next door or Scraps' mom, Miz Burke. I wish I didn't have to call nobody. I wish I could go on living here in this house like Earl and Grandma were still around.

I stop walking, one foot stuck in the air. What if I could keep it a secret? Well, I know I couldn't just bury Earl in the backyard. I hear the dirt settles in the rain and the police would find the body or dogs could dig it up. That creeps me out so I rub my arms and wiggle around like a cold wind hit my back.

I could take the body somewhere else. I never drove past the end of the driveway, but it don't seem that hard, I know alotta dumb people who can drive. But where could I take him?

I take another look at Earl. I try to pull up his pants. It ain't easy cuz there's crap all over and it makes me gag. The best I can do is put one towel over his butt and one over his head, and then I go call 911.

I tell the 911 lady my grandpa died. She starts to give me instructions for CPR, but I tell her it's no use. She asks if there's anyone else there and I say no, my grandma's gone. She says she's dispatching an ambulance, and I can just hear Earl yelling about how much it's gonna cost.

After I hang up, I go over to Earl's rolltop desk in the corner of the living room. It's real old, what Grandma called an antique, used to belong to Earl's grandpa. It has all kinds of little boxes Earl called pigeonholes. I reach into one and take out Earl's little red address book. It has lots of names and numbers and cross-outs and grease smudges. I flip through, thinking I might find Grandma's number there. I do, but it's the old apartment where we used to live before we came to live with Earl. It's been a few weeks since I've heard from her, she'll be calling me soon. I send out a message to her from my mind. Call me, Grandma, call me, call me.

I keep flipping through the little book and find Bobby Scudder's number. I guess he's Earl's best friend or only friend, but I hate that slobby stinking jerk. There's Nadine too, Earl's sister. Her page has lots of cross-outs too, not just numbers and addresses but last names. She's got a couple of ex-husbands and two grown kids. Her last name is Coombs now. Oregon is not so far away, she could be here tomorrow.

The idea makes me shiver, like when you touch your fillings with tin foil. Quite a few years ago, she spent part of a summer with us. She and Earl fought most the time, mainly over this house. She owns half of it, and she complained about Grandma and me living here rent-free. She's a real nasty bitch with orange hair and a big brown spot above her lip like a drop of poop. I'll do the right thing and call her, but not right now.

About twenty minutes later the ambulance pulls up but quiet, with no siren going, just the lights flashing. I run out to meet the ambulance people so they know they're at the right house. Two real young ladies in white coats, they're like teenagers, jump out of the ambulance. One has a blond ponytail shooting out of the top of her head like a drinking fountain, the other one is chewing a big wad of pink bubble gum, watermelon it smells like. When they see me, Ponytail Girl's eyes get big and sad and Watermelon, as brown as me, straightens up so she looks taller and walks kind of stiff. I lead them inside the house and into the bathroom. I stand in the hallway, waiting. It's kind of embarrassing, these young ladies and me and Earl with his pants down laying in his own poop, but they don't seem to mind. Maybe alotta people poop when they die, everything just lets loose.

It takes them like five minutes to check Earl out. Watermelon stands up and looks me in the eyes. "I'm sorry, there's nothing we can do. He has expired," she sez, which has to mean dead. "The coroner has to come before we can take the body away." She places her hand on my shoulder as light as a butterfly. I start crying then. I don't know what took me so long.

# twelve

SOME TIME MUST GO BY without me knowing it cuz next thing I know I'm sitting on the couch with Ponytail Girl, answering a bunch of questions while she fills out a paper. She asks do I live here and what is my relationship to Earl and how long has he been sick. I tell her about his Agent Orange and breathing problems. Then she asks what school do I go to and do I like my teachers. Some of the questions seem pretty dumb, but then I see she's stopped writing, she's just trying to make me feel better.

I hear someone drive up. I look out the window and see a cop climbing out of his cruiser. Crap, it's Officer Hackett. He's like assigned to our hood, and once he busted me for truancy at the mall on a day when I was suspended. First they kick me out of school, then they bust me for not being in school. He made a couple of home visits last spring to check if I was going to school most days I wasn't suspended. Seeing him now makes me realize I haven't seen him hanging around for awhile.

I open the door and he sez, "Hey R.D., I'm real sorry to hear about your grandpop."

"Yeah," I sez. "Me, too."

"Where's Grandmom?"

"I don't know."

"When do you expect her back?"

This catches me by surprise, him thinking Grandma is like just out for the evening. It gives me hope for one more night of freedom before CPS jumps me. "I don't know," I sez.

"Think she's at the Palace?"

I pick my words careful, cuz I don't want to be accused of lying later. "She likes going to the Palace, but I just don't know."

"You don't know much, do you, R.D.?" sez Hackett, trying for a lame joke. When I don't laugh, the tops of his ears and the tip of his nose turn pink.

"Where you been anyways?" I ask.

"Up in Sacramento. Motorcycle school." He's trying to hide it, but his ham face shows pride and shame all mixed together.

I make a big deal of looking out the window. "I don't see no motorcycle."

"Yeah, yeah, I'm working on it."

The doorbell rings and it's the coroner. It's another lady, not quite as young as the ambulance girls. She looks kind of surprised to be out, like her clothes are sort of thrown on and her hair is sticking up. I thought all coroners looked like Abraham Lincoln, tall, skinny, sad men in black suits and top hats, but maybe I'm thinking of funeral guys. She introduces herself as Leslie something, deputy coroner.

"Where's Phil?" Officer Hackett asks her.

"Out in Orosi. Another shooting."

"Gang related?"

"No, domestic violence, of sorts. Apparently this guy wanted a divorce and he and the wife went to their pastor for counseling. Pastor recommended reconciliation so the guy shot him."

They look at each other, blinking hard. The ambulance girls show Leslie into the bathroom, talking both at once. She's in there awhile and then she comes out and asks me alotta the same questions Ponytail Girl asked me and then, "Who's his doctor?"

"I don't know, but he's at the Veterans' Hospital."

"Way up in Palo Alto? Nobody local?"

I shrug. "Just the emergency room doctors a couple of times."

The corners of her mouth turn down as she writes on her form. "I'm reporting this as death by natural causes. There's no need for an inquest. Who's the next of kin?"

Officer Hackett is real quick to help out. "R.D.'s the deceased's step-grandson. His grandmom is out." He looks at me and sez, "You don't have any idea when she'll be back, R.D.?"

"Nope."

"What about the boy's parents?" asks the coroner, talking about me like I'm not even standing there.

"Mom's doing time, Dad's not in the picture," sez Hackett, like he knows everything about me.

The coroner looks at her watch and sighs. "I was on a date. Isn't there any way we can contact her? She doesn't have a cell phone?"

"Nope," I sez.

"You go on, Leslie," sez Officer Hackett. "I'll stick around."

Her head is still bent over her report. Her face sort of changes so I can tell she's happy to get out of here. "Which mortuary will the deceased be transported to?"

"I don't—"

"Silva's Funeral Home," Officer Hackett blurts out.

Leslie stops writing and looks up at him. "You sure?"

"Oh, yeah. Mrs. Silva and Mrs. Mitchell have been Bingo buddies down at St. Joseph's for years. They ran the linguesa booth together at the Our Lady of Fatima Festival since I was a little kid." He thinks he knows a lot about us, but his info is way old. Grandma hasn't played Bingo at the Catholic Church since the Palace opened up.

"Well Mike, there's a fifty-fifty chance you're right. If you're not, I guess it won't hurt to ship him off to Scagnetti's tomorrow morning." When she's all done filling out her papers she sez, "Good night," like that's going to happen, and leaves.

Officer Hackett calls up Silva's Funeral Home, asks to speak to Mrs. Silva, and when he mentions the name Rose Mitchell I'm surprised she doesn't ask who the hell that is, but I guess people who run funeral homes gotta remember alotta people if they expect to get them as business when they die.

The ambulance girls wheel a stretcher into the house to load up Earl. While they're getting him ready to go, Officer Hackett asks, "Is there someone you'd like to stay with until your grandmom gets home, R.D.?"

I shake my head slow and sad, pretending I'm like acting in a movie. "I need to be right here when she gets back."

"You'll be okay here alone? You're not afraid of death?"

"They're taking him away, right? If I get scared I can run across the street to the Burkes."

"I'll give Mrs. Burke a call right now, explaining the situation."

"No! I can take care of my—"

A call comes on Hackett's radio, and he holds his meaty hand up. The info is all in code but I know what it means— gangbangers are hitting it at the Oval, a park near here, and Hackett has to go in for backup. He sticks his thumbs in his belt and stares at the floor like he's thinking hard, then looks up at me again. "Well, I guess you've got the Burkes if you need anyone. Offer your grandmom my condolences."

I never heard of that but I know what he means. While I'm standing at the door watching him drive off, I got to take a couple of quick breaths like I've been holding my air without knowing it. By then the ambulance girls got Earl all zipped up in a plastic bag. They wheel him out the door and load him into the ambulance while I watch.

It's a pretty night. I look up at all the stars. They're just hanging up there like they always do. Then I stand in the street and watch the red taillights of the ambulance get farther away. At the end of our street the brake lights come on, then off, like it's Earl winking good-bye to me.

# thirteen

I GO BACK IN THE HOUSE. It's real quiet, too quiet. I try watching TV, but I can't find nothing good on. I'm staring at the pictures flashing on the screen without really seeing them. All I can think is what's gonna happen to me. It won't take the cops long to figure out Grandma's not around.

My stomach growls. I don't feel like eating, but I'm hungry at the same time. I find some leftover spaghetti Earl was keeping warm for me in the oven. It's the last spaghetti Earl made me that I'll ever eat. I look in the fridge and see we're out of milk. We're out of most things. Earl liked to shop on Friday mornings before the weekend.

I eat the spaghetti in front of the TV. Earl used to say it wasn't civilized to eat in front of the TV, but who's gonna stop me now? After awhile I turn off the TV, but for some reason I don't turn off the living room lights or the kitchen lights. It's like I'm trying to fill up the empty spaces Earl left behind with light.

I go to my room, kick off my shoes, and flop into my bed. If Earl was here, he'd poke his head in the door and remind me to take my shower. I hate to shower in the morning and get all cold with a wet head. But old Earl ain't going to poke his head in ever again. I doze off, but I'm wide awake again around one o'clock. I lay in the dark staring up at the ceiling till I can't stand it. I haul myself out of bed and start pacing around the house again.

I don't believe in ghosts, but Earl is here all right. I can feel him. Maybe if I turn around quick, I'll see him standing there, his sagging jeans hanging off his old flat butt, his hangdog look like he's weary of it all.

I'm sorry, Earl, I say to him in my mind. I'm sorry he's dead, but I'm also sorry his life wasn't so happy. He seemed okay when Grandma was around, but after she left, he went downhill. I wonder when the funeral is gonna be and where. Earl didn't have no church. I wonder who will come. The neighbors will, I guess, and his customers who read about it in the newspaper. I got to call Bobby and Nadine soon as I find out about it. I wonder if people will bring me some food and casseroles. That makes me feel kind of cheap so I say "I'm sorry, Earl," right out loud like he can hear me.

I get in bed again, but I lay awake and lay awake. I just slightly doze off, then jerk myself awake like I'm about to catch myself from falling off a cliff. Finally I get to sleeping real good and my alarm wakes me up. I whack it off and roll over. Man, I'm wiped. Whenever I feel tired from staying up all night, Earl calls me two or three times, and tries to yank me out of bed by the arm or legs, and if I still won't go, he lets me alone, calls the attendance lady, and sez I'm sick.

Then I remember Earl can't make the call, but for sure the school will let me stay home the day after Earl died. But then maybe they don't know Earl's dead. Officer Hackett could've told Officer Mendez, but then Officer Mendez is always at Buzz Middle and hardly gets a chance to hear stuff round the police station. Maybe if I go to school I can keep it a secret Earl died, but if I stay home Officer Mendez might come knocking at the door.

I jump up, run to the kitchen, look over the cereal cart. There's nothing left but Earl's crappy bran flakes. That's like eating sawdust and with no milk. I'll eat at school. I run back to my room, pick up my backpack which feels too heavy. I look inside, find Dominic's literature book and toss it out. Next to it is a jacket I don't recognize. It takes me a sec to think where it come from. I kick it aside and run out of my room as I hear the diesel engine of the school bus chugging down the street. I bolt out the front door, leap down the steps, then remember to lock the house. I open the front door, turn the lock, then slam the door. I run down the street, flagging the bus driver down.

# fourteen

DOMINIC DIDN'T MAKE IT on the bus, but Scraps did. I flop into the seat across the aisle from him.

He shakes the hair out of his face so I can see more than his needle nose for a change. "Hey, is everything cool?"

"Why wouldn't it be?"

"My mom saw them loading Earl up in the ambulance."

I look at Scraps like he's totally tripping. "Well then, she saw wrong."

"She saw the stretcher thingie come outta your house."

"They were gonna take him away, but then they got him breathing again."

Scraps' head jerks back like he got popped in the nose. "Whoa, he stopped breathing?"

"For a little bit, but I called 911 and the lady told me how to give him CPR, and I kept him going till they got there." This all rolls off my tongue easier than the truth cuz laying awake all night I saw it in my mind playing over and over like a movie.

"Serious, R.D., you saved his life?"

I nod slow. Scraps is really easy to lie to cuz he wants to believe me. He wants to believe we're so tight, I would never lie to him.

He opens his mouth to ask more questions, but I cut him off. "Hey, chill. I hardly got no sleep last night." I slump down against the window and close my eyes.

Next thing I feel a jolt—it's the bus pulling up at the loading zone. My stomach gurgles and growls. I head straight for the cafeteria, I don't care who sees me free-and-reduced, but then I hear a wild whoop clear across the yard and see Desiree is already there in the breakfast line. Damn, I don't wanna have to mess with her so I cut off in the other direction. I stand around chillin, listening to my stomach complain, when I see Desiree heading my way. She sees me seeing her so there's no getting away.

I thought she'd be pist, but she's got one big pretty smile for me like I never did nothing wrong. She wraps her arms around me and smashes her whole body up against mine and I hug her back. Water comes into my eyes it feels so good to be holding someone after all I been through. The whole time I'm thinking I gotta let go, I gotta let go, so I can hardly enjoy it. There ain't no PDAs allowed at Buzz Middle and we could get into trouble. They could give us discipline referrals and call home.

The girls in our school are the huggingest bunch you ever seen, even if Public Displays of Affection is against the rules.

This one Hugging Girl last year stood out in front of math class, squealed out your name and ran up and hugged you. I seen boys sometimes circling around her, walking on the grass, what we're not supposed to do, just to dodge her. She didn't just hug the guys neither, but all her little girlfriends, too.

I let go of Desiree first, she's like doing a little freak dance against me. Girls just don't know what they do to guys, the ho clothes they wear and how they act, or maybe Desiree does know. She's probably done it. I never have cuz I never knew a girl who would with me, but it looks like I got one now.

I wonder if it's as great as all the guys say. I know this one guy who sez too much gives him a headache and this other guy sez he got the crabs, these little spider things crawling up his butt. But if it goes right, it's supposed to be the best thing in the world.

"I heard you ditched yesterday," Desiree sez.

"Yeah," I sez, picturing myself walking off school grounds with both of her fries. Don't she even care how messed up that is?

"Once I ditched a whole month."

"Your mom didn't make you go to school?"

"I ran away." She touches the tip of her tongue to her lip, all proud of herself.

"You lived on the street?"

"Hell, no. I stayed at friends' houses. My mom didn't care."

Earl would care if I didn't come home at night. Oh Earl! Whole minutes can go by without me remembering he's gone. "I gotta go."

"I'll go with you."

"Naw, I gotta go by myself and it's gonna take me a long time."

She blinks. "You gotta do a number two, R.D.?"

"No!" This girl gets too personal.

"You wanna meet at the mall tomorrow?"

"I don't know, when?"

"About eleven? In front of the Fashion Mode?"

Seeing Desiree at the mall might be cool, at school she's just trouble. "I'll try to make it." I run across the yard and go stand in the breakfast line behind some big dude so tall and fat I gotta check twice to make sure he ain't a teacher.

I think I'm hiding real good, but then there's a tap on my shoulder. I turn around and snap, "Yeah, what?"

Jeanette's green eyes grow wide. She backs away on one foot.

"Sorry, sorry! I thought you was someone else."

"Did you get it done?"

"What done?" Then I remember. Castles—I was supposed to find pictures of them. "I didn't get around to it. I was busy."

"I had math homework and science and leadership posters to paint, and I still managed to get some stuff off the internet for our report." School is her whole life. She's so different from me she might as well be a Martian.

"I was dealing with a dead body, okay?" I don't know why I said that, maybe to shock her or cuz if I don't say out loud what's really wrong to at least one person I'll go crazy.

She shakes her head, short and quick. "Never mind. I'll do it."

"I'll go to the public liberry, okay? Tomorrow. It's right by my house." I keep going on and on, begging her to let me do homework. "I can bring the castle books to your house on Sunday."

"Don't say you're coming if you have no intention." Then she's gone, nothing left of her but the smell of Raspberries in the Sun body spray.

A shoulder knocks against mine. Desiree is standing there, her arms crossed, dogging Jeanette. "She was talking stuff about me."

"She don't even know you."

"I'll claw her eyes out."

"She don't want to fight you. Leave her alone."

Desiree stares at my face like a movie hard to get. "Why? What's she to you?"

"She's in my core class. We're in the same castle group."

"Yeah? Well, she better stay away from my man. I'll frickin kill her."

# fifteen

IN CORE we're just getting into our groups when a hall pass comes for me. Most kids love to get passes cuz it means you get out of class. Usually it's just to clear an absence with the attendance lady or talk to your advisor. Other times it can be real good like your mom left you lunch money in the student office or she's here to take you to the dentist and you don't have to go back to school for the rest of the day. No one ever left me no money and I haven't been to the dentist in years. Hall passes are never good for me.

I walk over to the office wondering what I'm getting busted for. It could be alotta things—jacking Sterling's jacket or Dominic's literature book or Desiree giving me PDAs in the yard. I got a feeling though it's much worse, like CPS coming to put me in a home.

There's a backup of kids waiting to see Bowan, some sitting in chairs in the halls, some in the rooms they use for holding tanks. The office should get one of those little machines the bakery has where you gotta tear off a little paper number so you know whose turn it is. I look around, but I don't know anyone except the 504 Anger Kid who got retained same as me. Number 504 means he can't help himself. He throws a chair at a teacher or cusses one out or slams her against the wall and bumps her head, it's not his fault. Officer Mendez just comes to the classroom and takes him out to chill in the office.

I take a seat in the chair next to him, not dogging him, but sneaking looks at him. He's a four-eyed, dumb-looking guy with orange hair and freckles and a moon face that flushes pink easy. He sneaks out of his seat and grabs one of those sticks you use to pick up trash with handles you squeeze at the top to work pinchers at the end. He gets back in his seat and starts swinging it around, not hitting nobody, just for something to do. Out in the yard the other kids make fun of him, try to get him angry so he'll charge them, so he's got to stay in the office before school and after school and break and lunch to keep him from getting in fights. He don't get sent to Merit Reform like other kids cuz like I sez, he don't have regular anger, he's got 504 Anger. It's hard to know what to do with a kid like him, just sit him in the office about half his life.

Mr. Bowan's office door opens and I must be special or something cuz he calls me in before the others. Miz Donaldson is in there too. I never seen her wear this purple skirt and the fluffy sweater that matches it. Come to think of it, I've never seen Miz Donaldson wear the same thing twice.

She sez, "You're saggin-and-baggin, R.D. Hike them up."

Mr. Bowan takes my backpack and dumps it out on a little table. There's just my flannel overshirt and binder. He begins shuffling through the binder, looking for gang signs. It's brand new, with new paper and tab dividers with nothing written on them and a pencil case with new pencils and pens Earl got me at the Wal-Mart for my fresh start.

"Where were you yesterday afternoon, R.D.?" Mr. Bowan asks. "Mrs. Stone marked you absent."

"I was there. She must've missed me."

Mr. Bowan rolls his bulging peanut M&M eyes. "Oh, come off it, R.D., we're not playing with you like we done—did—last year."

I bet old Mrs. Stone wouldn't swear I wasn't in science, but I ain't had no sleep and no food and I'm starting to miss Earl real bad. I drop my head and rub my eyes. "Okay. I was at the park."

"That's better. Did you go home last night?" asks Miz Donaldson.

"Course. I always go home at night."

"You sure?" sez Bowan, stretching his neck out and leaning into me. "Those are the same clothes you wore yesterday."

"And your grandpa called here looking for you," sez Miz Donaldson.

"He did?" I sit straight up! Earl's come back to life? He's not dead, he's recovering in the hospital? Wait a minute. "When?"

"About five," she sez. "He said you didn't come home on the bus and he was worried."

"Oh! Oh, you mean yesterday. I couldn't figure out . . ."

"How much school have you attended this year?" asks Bowan.

"Wait." Miz Donaldson holds up her palm. "You couldn't figure out what, R.D.?"

"Well, just that, um, Earl's in the hospital. The ambulance come last night cuz he had trouble breathing. You can ask Scraps—Gilbert—if you don't believe me," I sez, even though I told him the exact opposite story. Earl sez lying is like a spider spinning a web to catch itself.

"Oh, I'm sorry to hear it," sez Miz Donaldson. "That explains why there's been no answer at your house. We've been trying to call all morning."

"You can't miss any more school," sez Bowan.

"Goodness no," sez Miz Donaldson with a chuckle. "At this rate we'll have to furnish you with your own parking space here."

"I won't ditch again, I promise. Only please don't call my house no more. My grandma has enough worries with Earl sick. I'm going to help her out by doing my work and staying out of trouble."

"You see that you do." Mr. Bowan offers his hand and I shake it, and then Miz Donaldson offers her hand and I shake it, and then I walk out of there free as a bird.

# sixteen

WHEN I GET BACK to core class, Miz Trueblood is saying something about prefixes, roots, and suffixes. There's an assignment on my desk, a kind of chart thing. I sort of see what's she's talking about, but not exactly. I try to break down the first word, "mortuary." *Thunk!* A huge spitball hits me in the ear, coming from Dominic's direction.

He's got a wad of shredded paper in his cheek the size of a golf ball. His handiwork is hanging in gobs off the bulletin boards, posters, and cupboards. Miz Trueblood don't see any of this, that's how new teachers are. They're so busy smiling and teaching their shiny new lesson plans that they don't see nothing.

I try to ignore Dominic and do what I'm supposed to do. I look up the root *mort*. *Mort* means dead. Earl is *mort*, laying on the stone cold bathroom linoleum, his gray tongue sticking out, crap all over. The bell rings. All the kids are yelling to their friends and laughing and pushing toward the door, but I just sit there.

"Can I help you with something, R.D.?" Miz Trueblood's voice is so sudden and close to my ear, I jerk like I've been caught doing something bad.

"This root thing don't make no sense."

"Doesn't make any sense. Why?"

"*Mort* means dead and *ary* means place, so a mortuary must mean a place for dead people, but I know that's called a cemetery."

"Very good, R.D. A cemetery is where the dead are buried, and a mortuary is where bodies are prepared for burial."

"What do you mean 'prepared'?"

"The funeral arrangements are made, the coffin is selected, and well, you know what embalming is, don't you?"

"I guess so." Then I shake my head. "No. What is it?"

"It's a little gruesome to talk about. The blood is replaced with embalming fluid to preserve the body for the funeral."

"They're going to do that to Earl?" I'm so surprised, I'm nearly shouting.

"Who's Earl?"

"My grandpa. He's awful sick. He's had Agent Orange a long time."

"You mean, he was *exposed* to Agent Orange. Ah, that's too bad. A lot of Vietnam vets came home affected by it, including my boyfriend's father." She looks over my work and shakes her head. "R.D., you've got prefixes in the root column and suffixes in the prefixes column. Weren't you here when I showed the class how to do this type of assignment?"

"I got suspended for three days. Remember?"

"I remember. Why three days? Why not just one?"

"I don't know. Mr. Bowan just wanted to get rid of me. But if the school really wanted to get rid of me, why did they flunk me?"

"You're *repeating* eighth grade?"

"Well, yeah. So is just about everybody in the class."

Miz Trueblood lets out a puff of air that ends in "ha," a kind of short laugh. "That explains a lot! You haven't failed, R.D., the system has failed *you!* You're certainly bright enough."

"I never do my work, Miz, but this year I'm gonna. I got to or Mr. Bowan is going to send me to the county boot camp."

"Mr. Bowan!" She crosses her arms and scowls. With her jelled hair going every which way, she looks like a mad rooster. "I hope he knows that poor defenseless little girl's brains would have been spilled all over the sidewalk if it wasn't for you."

I nod, trying to look serious, but laughing inside. Desiree—defenseless! As I'm clamping my binder shut, my eye catches the word "mortuary" and something twists inside me. "Uh, how do you find out when the mortuary is done and all ready to have the funeral?"

"The family makes the arrangements, R.D. Chooses the church, the coffin, the final resting place—everything. When the time comes, your grandma will do all that with your parents' help." Her row of gold bracelets jingles as she pats my arm. "It's not for you to worry about."

"Right." I try slinging my backpack over my shoulder, but it slips down my arm like I don't have the strength to hoist it all the way up.

# seventeen

I TURN THE KNOB on the front door. It's locked. I yell, "Hey Earl, let me in." That's how dumb I am thinking about doing Earl's funeral and at the same time forgetting he's dead.

I go around the back, but before I get there I know that's no good either. Earl was always careful about locking the place up. I know there's no window open I can crawl through. I got to break into my own house. I get a hubcap laying around in the yard and swing it at the window above the sink. *Crash!* Man, it's loud, but people in my hood don't pay no attention to stuff.

I drag a car seat over to the opening I've made, my stomach rumbling. There's got to be something in that kitchen for me to eat, I promise I don't care what. I ate cafeteria slop for lunch and was glad to get it, but it still wasn't enough. I climb up on the car seat and start to yank the jagged pieces of glass out of the window frame. I slice my thumb and it hurts like hell.

I watch the bright blood oozing out, thinking about how when I was little, my grandma always made a big fuss when I got hurt. She'd give me some cookies to make it better, and—I don't remember this, but she told me—once when I skinned both knees she gave me two cookies and I pressed them on my knees and said, "Grandma, the cookies aren't making me feel no better." She told me that story every time I got hurt, like I never heard it before.

Blood's dripping all over my flannel shirt so I take it off and wrap it around and around my hand like a kind of glove. Then I go after the broken glass some more. I bail through the window head first. I feel some glass scrape against my shin, tearing into my jeans. I land in a sink of dirty dishes and I have to remember why the sink isn't empty and scrubbed clean.

I open the fridge out of habit, knowing nothing is there. There's just two heels in the bread wrapper, which I would never eat before, but they're good enough now. I open the cupboard Earl used to call the pantry. It's full of junk I never noticed before: Bisquick, cornmeal, flour, macaroni, spaghetti, sugar, molasses, vegetable oil, baking soda, and little stuff like cinnamon, garlic powder, salt, pepper, vanilla. All kinds of food, and none I know how to make so I can eat it. Earl always did want to teach me how to cook.

I take the tie twist off the package of macaroni. It's called elbow macaroni, I guess because the pieces are curved like little elbows. I pop a few macaronies in my mouth and try to crunch, but they're hard as plastic so I spit them in the sink. I pour a big tumbler of water thinking that will fill me up. I'm gulping it down when the phone rings.

It's a lady with an old wobbly voice asking, "May I speak to Mrs. Rose Mitchell?" It sounds like one of those people trying to sell stuff over the phone, so I hang up. The phone rings again and it's the same lady. "Hello? We were disconnected. It's imperative that I speak to Mrs. Mitchell."

She wants to play, I'll play. "What's so imperative about it?"

"This is Estelle Silva from Silva's Funeral Home."

"Oh! Sorry, sorry, Miz Silva. I thought you was one of those people trying to sell stuff over the phone."

There's a pause. "Mrs. Mitchell, please."

"She can't come to the phone right now. She's not here. I mean, she is here, but she's sleeping."

"To whom am I speaking?"

"This is R.D., her grandson. The doctor gave her stuff to make her sleep cuz she's a mess, you know, cuz you know, Earl died."

"Of course. We have the loved one here with us. When is she coming in to make the arrangements?"

I could say Grandma is too messed up to come, and come myself, but how would I get there? I know where Silva's Funeral Home is. I seen it lots of times, a couple of blocks away from the high school. It's too far to walk and my skateboard is broke. I look out the front window and the funniest thing is I see Earl's pickup. Well, who's stopping me? I've backed up and down the drive hundreds of times. Why not go a little farther? I gotta wait till dark though, when no one can see me.

"Hello?" sez the wobbly voice.

"Yes, Miz Silva, I'm just thinking. How about tonight?"

"I'm not here after regular business hours, but I can have one of our counselors speak with her."

I went to church camps with counselors. It's weird to think of those guys at a funeral chapel. "That would be good, Miz Silva, real good."

"In that case, I'll make the appointment for seven o'clock."

"How about eight? It doesn't get dark till eight. I mean, uh . . . Grandma can't face the daylight, not after Earl died."

"Eight o'clock, then. She'll be consulting Mr. Walstein, Charles Walstein."

"Thanks. She'll be there."

After I hang up, I stare at the phone, thinking now would be a good time to call Nadine and Bobby, but I don't feel like talking to Bobby. He'll call CPS for sure. He can wait till I know when the funeral is and so can Nadine. She'll be coming down from Oregon soon enough to kick me out of this house.

# eighteen

I GO DOWN THE HALL into Earl's room, which is kind of creepy, grab the truck keys out off the little green saucer on top of his chest of drawers, and run out. I stare at the truck out the front window, squeezing the keys so tight they dig into my palm. I know if I break some traffic law I don't know about, I'll get pulled over and get found out. I'll go real slow. I'll only take back streets. I wouldn't even know how to get on the freeway.

I put on Earl's John Deere cap and his old jeans jacket. I get a strong whiff of him: cigarettes, motor oil, stale BO. I wonder how long Earl's smells are gonna hang around.

I turn out all the lights in the house. As I head toward the pickup I sort of hunch up my back and bend my legs like Earl did. I want to run to the safety of the cab, but I know that wouldn't look like Earl. When I finally get there, I slide low in the seat, my heart pounding. I think of all the stuff I have to remember. Release the hand brake, stomp on the clutch, push the stick into reverse. My hand is shaking when I turn the key. The motor roars like something alive. Am I really going to do this?

I back her out real slow. The crunching gravel is like yelling at me don't do it. I wait at the end of the drive, looking up and down and up and down for cars, for skaters, for little kids, for dogs and chickens and rolling balls and little Hmong grandpas. The coast is clear so I pull out, let the clutch out too fast, and kill the motor. Hand shaking, I start her up again and peel out with an awful screech, laying a patch without even trying.

At the end of our street, I have to turn left onto a busier street, but with no street light and lots of cars whizzing by, I don't dare. A car pulls in behind me, which really gets me sweating. When the guy honks, I just turn right, cutting in front of another car that's suddenly there in my way. That guy slams on his brakes and lays on his horn too. There's sure alot you gotta watch out for when you're driving.

It takes a long time to get to Silva's Funeral Home just making right turns, and I kill the motor a couple more times at stop signs, but eventually I make it. There's lots of cars in Silva's parking lot and some more on the street. Jeez, are all these people making funeral plans? Was there a big train wreck or something?

I have to park a long ways away because I don't know how to parallel park so I got to find a long piece of curb to nose dive into. I walk back to Silva's and follow some people inside. They look me down and up like I don't belong there, even sniff the air a little bit, one old lady staring hard at

Earl's cap. Then I remember Grandma saying to take my cap off inside places, so I slip it off.

A stooped guy in a black suit with a couple of long hairs combed from one side of his bald head to the other comes up to me and asks, "Are you here for the James Willard visitation or for Roberto Ortiz?"

Visitation—that's what they call it? I can't remember the name Miz Silva give me, but I know it started with a W. "Willard," I sez.

He leads me to like a big living room, with all kinds of sofas and a fireplace, but I see it's fake, and mounds and mounds of flowers, so many you can hardly breathe without flower smell tickling the inside of your nose.

Then I see him—a dead guy all propped up in his coffin like death just caught him sudden-like, right in the middle of a sit-up. He's real old with a tense smile, the kind you make just before a fart. He's got on makeup and hair spray and glasses like he fell asleep reading.

What's he need glasses for now? I remember at one of those church camps they said when you die you see God. Would God be all blurry if this guy didn't have his glasses?

"Doesn't Jim look good?" one lady whispers, sniffing into a wad of Kleenex and staring at the dead guy.

I don't think he looks good. He looks just awful, and I feel sorry for Earl if they're going to make him look that bad. Who is this guy? Is he just kind of a display like in Wal-Mart so you know what you're getting?

One old lady is taking it real hard. She's sobbing and carrying on and moaning, "My Jim, oh my Jim, he's gone."

So now I get it. A visitation is visiting a dead guy one last time before he gets buried. I'm in the wrong room. I don't dare leave, it would be like rude. So I just sit there and wait until some other people get up to leave and I go out with them.

They go out the front door but I stop in the lobby. The guy with the long hairs pasted over his bald head sez, "Can I help you, sir?"

"I got stuck in the wrong room."

"So sorry, sir. This way, please." He leads me to another kind of living room with another group of people crying over another dead guy.

"No," I whisper. "I'm not here for no visitation at all. I'm here to see about my grandpa's funeral, Earl Mitchell."

"Oh! Well then, I'm your counselor, Charles Walstein." He looks behind me. "We were expecting your grand-mother."

"She's . . . she can't get out of bed."

"It does happen." He shakes his head sadly. "She must be grief stricken."

"Uh yeah, grief stricken. She asked me if I could come over first to see about things, then tell her what you said."

"Very well." He leads me to a kind of showroom, not of cars like a dealership, not TVs like Circuit City, but coffins—he calls them caskets. I pick out the shiniest one, a copper one he calls "Cashmere beige with a champagne velvet interior."

We go to his office and he offers me a chair, and he sits down at his big desk and starts filling out a paper. "Does your grandfather belong to a church?"

"No sir." I know some people in Goldhurst think people

who aren't Christians are the devil, but Mr. Walstein doesn't seem to care.

"Will our chapel be an acceptable place for the service?"

"Sure, that would be great."

"Is he a veteran of a foreign war?"

"Yeah, Vietnam."

"I'll contact the VA for a flag then."

I imagine Earl's coffin draped with the old stars and stripes, just like a war hero and think he would really like that.

Then he asks a bunch more questions about hairdressing and hearse rental. Each time I answer, I catch him sneaking peeks at my bare knee poking out of my jeans. There's spots of blood trailing down one pant leg from where I cut myself on the kitchen window.

Finally he sez, "You seem to have expensive taste, young man. Your grandma might want to keep the price down. Now, the final resting place. Will it be the Goldhurst City Cemetery?"

"Uh . . . yeah." Price? Oh God, you got to *pay* for a funeral—I got to pay? How am I gonna do that?

He slides the paper across the desk to me and stands. "Here's the estimate. Can you bring your grandmother over here tomorrow morning to make the final decisions, say ten o'clock?"

I have to stop and think: Tomorrow is Saturday. No school. "Okay, we'll be here."

"I'll tell Mrs. Silva then." He holds out his hand to shake, but I pretend I don't see it cuz I don't want to touch it in case he's been touching dead guys.

I don't dare look at the paper until I get in the truck. I
turn on the cab light and take in the bad news:

| | |
|---|---|
| Casket | $3,995 |
| Velvet interior | 199 |
| Pillow | 56 |
| Embalming | 395 |
| Casketing fee | 329 |
| Memorial cards | 125 |
| Hearse rental | 125 |
| Cemetery plot | 2,250 |
| Grave digging | 495 |

There's a bunch of other stuff too. My eyes slide down to
the total: $12,825. Now I see why that guy was staring at the
hole in my jeans. I shut the cab light off and lean back in the
dark. Finally I start the truck and head home.

The house is dark and lonely. When I open the door, it
seems to sigh, like it's full of ghosts. I go over to Earl's big
rolltop desk and look through all the pigeonholes. I need to
find out how much money he has in the bank. They won't let
me take it out, I know, but Silva's must have some way of getting money out of the bank accounts of dead people. Alotta
old people must die alone, with no one to make their funeral.

All of Earl's car-fixing records are in a neat cardboard file
box under his workbench, but his desk is a mess. Finally I
find what I'm looking for—a kind of letter he gets from the
bank every month that says how much money he has in his
account. It's not much, a couple of hundred bucks and I
know he's got no savings.

What am I gonna tell Mrs. Silva tomorrow? Maybe I shouldn't have ordered the champagne copper model, maybe Earl can't even afford the cheapest. Poor people can't even afford to die.

I know you don't have to be buried, you can get burned up into ashes—cream-something. I'm not even sure Earl can afford that.

My stomach growls so I go looking in the fridge for about the hundredth time. There's pickle relish, mustard, ketchup, horseradish, mayo, salad dressing, and way in the back, three beers. Three beers.

"Is there anybody here gonna stop me?" I shout out. Then I remember the big hole in the window over the sink. I look over my shoulder as if someone's out there watching me. Then I take out the beer.

I don't like the taste of beer, but I pop one open and guzzle it down. It's a pretty tall one and it makes me feel full. Just as I'm starting on the second one, I get the idea to check the freezer. There's food in there all right—a whole chicken. I take it out and yell at it, "How do I make you so I can eat you?"

The cold burns my fingers so I let it drop. When it hits the linoleum it shakes the house. I kick it. It hurts my foot, but it's so funny sliding across the floor I have to laugh. I go over and kick it again. I kick it and kick it till my toe throbs. I kick it until I cry. Doesn't anyone care about me? Won't anyone feed me? I'm all alone and I can't even bury Earl.

I pour the rest of the second beer down the sink, pop open the third can and pour it down too. I found out I'm just like Earl—a sad drunk. I don't know how he could stand it. I'd rather be no kind of drunk at all.

# nineteen

I DON'T HAVE THE NERVE to drive in broad daylight, so I borrow Scraps' board to get to Silva's, and I hide it in the bushes. I pull open the big heavy doors, wondering if they can have me arrested for ordering up a big funeral I can't pay for, like eating in a restaurant when you got no money. This is probably my last day of freedom anyways. I'm surprised Officer Hackett hasn't come to find me out already.

Inside it's dark and cool and real quiet with nobody around. I wonder if those two dead guys who had their visitations last night are still around. Maybe after everyone goes home at night, they climb out of their coffins and party together. Maybe they let Earl in on the fun.

"You're early," sez a deep voice right in my ear, and I about jump out of my skin. It's Mr. Walstein. "Sorry, son. I didn't mean to startle you." He looks behind me. "Where's Mrs. Mitchell?"

"She wouldn't come."

"Oh?"

"She wouldn't come and I couldn't make her." I'm acting again, making my voice strong and shaky, swiping at my eyes. I look down, notice I slept in my clothes again, the same damn holey, bloody jeans, and I feel the heat rising in my face. "The truth is, Mr. Walstein, I think she's too embarrassed to come see Miz Silva. We can't afford all that funeral stuff you wrote down on the paper."

"Yes, I know, R.D. I ran a credit check on your grandfather this morning. Don't worry. We'll work something out. Come into my office. Mrs. Silva isn't here yet, but we can get started." He places an arm around my shoulder, wriggles his nose a little, then lets go quick like I got germs or something. He takes a couple of quick steps ahead of me. At his big desk he looks over some papers and sez, "I see Mr. Mitchell's house is jointly owned by a Mrs. Nadine Coombs."

"That's his sister. She lives in Oregon."

"And she'll be coming down for the services?"

"I guess. The truth is, I—we—haven't called her yet. We thought we'd wait and plan the funeral first."

"I see. Well, maybe your grandmother will want to call her sooner than that. If Mrs. Coombs is going to sell the house, perhaps that's a way to raise revenue for funeral expenses."

"That won't work. Me and Grandma are planning to keep living in the house if Nadine will let us."

"Do you happen to know if your grandfather left a will?"

"I looked—me and Grandma looked—for one where he

kept his important papers, but we didn't find one. What will we do, Mr. Walstein?"

"Well, here's one idea. We participate in a service the city provides for people who die without kin or whose family can't afford to bury them. The loved one is cremated, the ashes are tagged with identification and placed in a plastic container. The ashes are then stored in the coroner's office until there's enough containers to fill a wooden casket, and then the casket is buried in a vault in the city cemetery."

I picture Earl's sorry ashes like sand in a kid's bucket, and a whole bunch of other buckets of people—people no one loved—all shut away in a vault. "I'm not so sure. That sounds like a cheap thing to do to poor Earl."

"Here's another alternative. Have you considered anatomical gifting?"

"What's that?"

"It's donating the body to science."

"Like having scientists look Earl over to see what the Agent Orange done to him so they can help other people with it? Earl would really like that."

"I don't mean anything so specific. Mostly it's universities that need cadavers for their anatomy classes."

"For people studying to be doctors?" This seems not as important as studying Agent Orange. If Earl's going to give over his guts I would like to have the pros working him over.

"Not exactly medical students. Any student enrolled in an anatomy class."

"Would they make jokes about him and dress him up and stuff?"

"Not at all. His remains would be treated with the utmost respect, I assure you."

"How much would it cost?"

"That's the good news, R.D. Not a cent. The university pays us for storage and shipping. What do you think?"

I hear the door creak open. There's a tiny lady standing in the doorway as stiff as death. She's dressed all in black, holding a cloth in her arms like a baby.

"Ah, Estelle, there you are. This is R.D. Mitchell. R.D., this is Mrs. Silva."

She steps forward, sniffs the air like I'm not good enough to be in the same room with her. "Don't get up," she sez in a kind of hard tone which means I should've. She speaks with a heavy accent, kind of like Spanish but I know it's something else.

"Mrs. Mitchell couldn't make it again this morning," sez Mr. Walstein.

Mrs. Silva pulls the other chair a little ways from me and sits. When she's all sunk in the cushions her tiny feet don't even touch the floor.

"You're friends with my grandma, Miz Silva," I sez, pouring on the charm. "Remember you and her used to play Bingo at St. Joseph's?"

"Ah, yes. Rose Mitchell. She switched cards on me once, when I wasn't looking."

"Not my grandma!"

"Oh, yes it was. I always remember my numbers and those numbers they called out were not mine." Her eyes are crinkly and her face goes soft. Then I get it. Grandma switching

85

the cards was a nice thing. "Oh, she did not give me a big win, only a few dollars, but she never would admit to switching those cards, and we laughed about it for weeks."

"R.D. has about decided on anatomical gifting if his grandmother agrees." Mr. Walstein shows me a whole list of universities Earl can go to. I choose the University of California cuz Earl lived in California all his life. Mr. Walstein gives me a paper to take home for Grandma to sign. I'll just forge it—I done that alotta times to papers the school sends home—and I'll drop it off later.

Mrs. Silva leans toward me and hands me the cloth she's been holding. I see that it's an American flag, all folded up in a triangle. "The VA sent this over this morning. You may keep it as a tribute."

"Thanks." My eyes water up as I play in my mind like a movie, this flag fluttering in the breeze draped over the big gleaming cashmere beige copper coffin I picked out. It's a bright sunny day in the cemetery and hundreds of people are there paying their last respects to Earl. Soldiers in uniform are standing by and they give Earl a 21-gun salute. I don't know how you get one of those, but I seen it in a movie once.

Mr. Walstein opens a desk drawer and sez, "Here are Mr. Mitchell's private possessions." He hands me a plastic bag. In it are Earl's glasses, watch, and wallet.

"Thanks." I stare at the wallet like I can see through it. Please God, let there be money in there.

Mr. Walstein walks me to the door. I plan to step away from him so I won't have to shake hands with him, but he steps away from *me,* like I been around worse things than dead guys. "Thanks, Mr. Walstein. I'm sorry about all the trouble we've caused you."

"It's our pleasure, R.D. Mrs. Silva is glad to return a favor to an old friend."

After Mr. Walstein goes back inside, I can hardly keep from running. I wanna get away fast to see what's in that wallet. I find Scraps' board where I hid it in the bushes and take off flying down the sidewalk toward the McDonald's on the other side of the high school. At a red light I get a chance to peek inside the wallet. There's bills in it, all right, five of them. A one, a one, a one, a five, and a ten. *A ten!* I'm gonna eat!

I'm so happy I can hardly stand it, but there's a nagging voice at the bottom of my excitement. I try not to pay attention to it, but it just gets louder and louder till I gotta listen. Eighteen dollars would buy a whole lot more at the grocery store, even though it wouldn't be all hot and tasty like McDonald's. I stand in front of the place one foot on the board, one on the sidewalk thinking. I'll just get fries.

Turns out they don't even got fries. Not till eleven o'clock and it's only 10:15. I order two hash browns. They're gone in four bites, and I'm not a bit fuller than I was before I ate them.

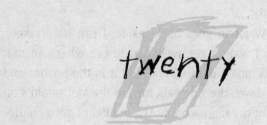

# twenty

I SKATE OVER to Wong's Market. I don't see no place to stash Scraps' board so I flip it up and tuck it under my arm. I pull a shopping cart out of the row, set the board in it. I never pushed a shopping cart and it feels funny, like I'm a kid playing house.

I must look funny too cuz this guy who's stacking up big brown sacks of potatoes sez, "Doing the grocery shopping for your mama?"

"Yes sir," I sez, and I see that he's not really a sir, but a young guy not much older than me. He's got black hair and a scruffy beard he can't quite grow. The plastic tag on his green apron sez "Arnie." He's setting up a sign: Russet potatoes, 10 pounds, 99¢.

"What's wrong with them?" I ask.

"Nothing's wrong with them. They're on sale this week."

"Yeah? McDonald's charges more for just this much potatoes." I cup my hands.

The Arnie guy laughs. "You know why it's called fast food, right?" He nods toward the bags of potatoes. "These take some work and time."

"How much work and time?"

"Depends on how you cook them. The easiest is to bake them. That takes an hour. Your mom is making you cook too?"

"She's never home." I lift a bag of potatoes off the pile and put them in the cart. It's real heavy, a whole lot of food. "What kind of pan do you use?"

"No pan. Just set them on the rack and turn the oven to 400 degrees. Oh, and jab them with a fork a couple times so they won't explode."

I laugh. The guy must think I'm so dumb I'll believe anything.

Oranges are $2.99 for a five-pound bag and apples are $1.99 for two pounds. I take apples cuz they're less money. Then I go to the butter case to buy the kind of cheap spread Earl bought. Next I look for bread. I pick up a loaf and then I see it's almost three dollars! I put it back and find the one Earl buys. It's 79¢. How can they cost so different when they look about the same?

Next is cereal. My favorite—Cocoa Puffs—is almost four dollars for a little box. There's bags as big as dog chow called Frosty Flakes for $1.98, so I get that. Now milk. It's way expensive, at $4.60 a jug. I used to drink two a week, but I gotta cut down. I get peanut butter and a little jar of grape jelly. I like strawberry jam better, but it's twice as much. Now I go for one little treat.

This is my lucky day. Mountain Dew is on sale, a twelve-pack for three dollars. Let's see, that's four cans for a dollar—a quarter a can. Whoa, it's a dollar in the soda machines at school. Rip-off! I add everything up one more time. Even without tax on food it's over eighteen dollars. Busted! I gotta put something back. I like apples the least, but that big bag of apples is a lot of food, compared to the little jar of jelly which costs almost as much. I hate having my peanut butter sandwiches naked so I decide to put back my lovely Mountain Dew.

I watch ladies roll huge baskets of food up to the checkout—frozen pizzas, big hunks of meat, ice cream, cookies, orange juice. What does it feel like to just go into a store and buy anything you want? I put my stuff on the conveyor belt, pay my money, and collect my change.

A pretty girl about my age asks if I need help to my car. I sure wish I had Earl's truck. Then the girl gives me a weird kind of scared look, and I realize she's looking at my weird kind of scared look and copying me. How do I get all this stuff home? "Uh, you got a box I can have?" I spread my arms. "About this big?"

She goes in the back of the store and brings me back a big ole box that sez Maxi Pads on it. I pack all my food in the box, carry it out of the store, and set it on Scraps' board. On my way home, I about break my back bending over pushing it, but I don't care, I got food. When I turn on my street I see Scraps and Dominic hanging out. Scraps is real happy to see his board come back, I been gone a long time.

When I lift the box of groceries off it, Dominic sez, "Man, you must have a real heavy period this month."

"I had to bring home the groceries in something."

"You never bought no groceries before," sez Scraps.

"Earl can't do it," I sez. "He's too sick."

"I wouldn't ever buy no groceries," sez Dominic. "That's women's work."

"What did ya get?" Scraps leans over my box, his hair swinging over his face so I can only see his nose. He paws through my food and sez, "Aw, nothin good."

"Hey, get out of there!" I butt him away with my shoulder, but I know what he means—chips and soda and ice cream. You can't be thinking about that kind of food when you only got sixteen dollars to feed yourself.

# twenty one

I DON'T EXPECT to see Desiree cuz I'm real late to the mall. The only person hanging out in front of Fashion Mode is a short lady standing next to a stroller. She's got a squirmy baby peeking over her shoulder like a monkey. Another little kid is climbing the garbage can, jumping off it, and knocking into people. The lady looks one way, then the other, like she's waiting for someone. Her face has a crushed look like she don't really expect that person to show. That's what makes me realize it's Desiree. Then she sees me and her painted-on eyebrows shoot up like the golden arches, only brown.

"About time, R.D.!" She's got her big, bright smile on and I think that's what I like best about her. She never gets pist no matter what I do. She puts out her free arm to hug me and I hug her back, but then she goes all stiff like she doesn't want me close so I back off.

"This here is André," she sez, bouncing the monkey on her shoulder. She digs her fingers into his ribs and he kind of squirms and laughs through his nose, making a big green booger pop in and out of one nostril like a worm going in and out a hole. "These are my nephews and niece, Luz's kids." She points to the stroller. There's a sleeping baby in there I didn't notice, all wrinkly-like, brand new. "That's Belle and that's Hector." She points to the hyper kid who's now squatted down, eating spilled popcorn off the floor.

We head into Fashion Mode. "Luz," Desiree calls out to this big lady with blonde streaks in her black hair and a big ole Raiders tat across the top of her boobs. Luz is carrying a whole armload of little ho bag dresses, what she couldn't get her big toe into.

Luz looks me up and down and makes some little sniffing sounds. I can tell she don't like me right off the bat. She has just a few rings of skin where her neck should be, but worst of all there's a real mean look to her. How a guy would ever get close enough to her to make a baby—three babies— well, some dudes ain't so particular. It makes me proud how cute and smiley Desiree is.

"Hey, me and R.D. are gonna hang out awhile." Desiree tries to hand the monkey over to Luz.

She don't take him, but the monkey knows his mama and reaches out and clings to her neck. She turns on Desiree with a look like she's just come down with mad cow disease. "You're dumping the kids on me when I don't got a moment's peace to shop?"

Desiree don't say nothing, just makes her smile stretch

out so it's a little pleading and a little guilty, her big brown eyes peeking around the two jelled ropes of hair dangling in her face.

Luz turns on me. "You gonna buy her something?"

"Uh . . . I don't got no money."

"You don't got no money or you don't got no money to spend on her? You know you owe her something."

"He don't." Desiree's smile goes from bright to just brave.

"That ain't what you told me," sez Luz.

I get hot in the face thinking what Desiree must've said about me. "I wanna get her something, but—" I take Earl's wallet out of my back pocket. "See? Empty."

Desiree takes the wallet out of my hand and runs her thumb over the tooling, worn smooth with age so you can barely read it. I was just a little kid when Grandma had it made special for Earl at the Tulare County Fair. "Earl? Ain't he your grandpa? You're bad, R.D."

"He gave it to me. To buy groceries. That's why I was late."

I try to stuff it in my pocket, but then Luz snatches it from me and holds it out of my reach. She sets the monkey down between her feet and starts going through the wallet, blocking me with her meaty shoulder. She holds up a Discover card and hoots, "Oh, girlfriend, can we ever have fun with this!"

"Come on, you can't use someone else's credit card."

"You can. Just say you're Earl," sez Luz. "There's an ID in here."

"I look like a old grandpa?"

Luz checks out Earl's driver's license, looks at me, looks at Earl's license, looks at me again. "Kind of." She puts the card back. She don't look so mean no more. She's probably just playing with me. Then she pulls out another card. "This don't need no ID."

She closes her hand over the card before I can see it, then tosses the wallet back to me. I fumble it, my hands kind of shaky, and by the time I get a good grip, she's stepping over the monkey, heading toward the door. The monkey sees his mom leaving without him and starts crying. The baby wakes up and starts crying. The circle rack of clothes Hector's been climbing tilts and slowly sags to the floor.

"Where's she going?" I ask Desiree.

# twenty two

DESIREE BENDS OVER to pick up the monkey. She hands him to me. Jeez, I don't want him. I set him down on his fat, bowed legs. He walks two steps and then sits back on his padded butt and howls some more.

"Desiree, tell me! What's she got?"

"I don't know. An ATM card, I guess." Her voice is muffled cuz she's busy hauling Hector out of all the dresses he spilled. She swats his butt a couple of times and now all three kids are howling. She swoops up the monkey and starts for the door. Hector is so mad he won't walk, so she's gotta drag him. "Come on, get the stroller."

"I ain't pushing no stroller."

"You want your share of the cash, don't you?"

"My share? She can't use an ATM card without a pin."

"Luz is good at figuring them things out."

I'm staring at the screaming baby, its face all angry and spotted red. It's so tiny it can hardly make a sound yelling its loudest. I notice its head is kind of pointy like it had a rough time making its way into the world. Once when Grandma got sloppy drunk she told me my mom had to work at pushing me out two whole days. She almost died of it. She was only fourteen and my dad was only thirteen, the boy next door. After his folks found out Yolanda was pregnant by him, they moved away in the night.

Desiree gets behind the stroller and sez, "You take the boys."

I grab Hector's hand, he ain't so bad, already stopped crying, but the monkey won't let go of Desiree so she's gotta lug him and push. We make our way through the mall, people dogging us, like all these kids are my fault.

"Where's Mr. Luz?"

"What?"

"A dude's been hangin round her, I can tell."

"They broke up."

"He seen his new kid yet?"

"That's why they broke up. He sez she ain't his. Course she is. Her and Hector are."

I figure I should shut up, but then I blurt out, "What about the monkey—I mean what's-his-name?" I point to the kid grabbed onto her shoulder.

"André? Rich Boy comes and goes. He's no good. Out gangbanging every night. That's why Luz would kill me if she found out why I got in that fight first day of school. She hates gangs."

"What kind of name is Rich Boy? I bet he's so rich he don't even pay a thing to his kid."

"Luz can take care of herself. She's got a good job at

Lucky's Steak House. Another couple months she'll be twenty-one and can work in the bar. Cocktail waitresses make bank."

We see Luz up ahead waiting her turn at the ATM machine. By the time we get to her, she's already punching in numbers.

"What are you trying?" asks Desiree.

"Duh! I'm trying Earl." She punches in the numbers, but it's a no-go.

"Does he got a dog?" Luz asks me.

"How much you taking out?"

"Just a hundred. I'll give you forty."

"Whoa, he's my grandpa."

"I'm doing all the work, and there's more of us. Tell me the damn dog's name."

We don't got a dog, but I sez, "Spot."

After that she keeps asking me questions and keeps try-ing stuff: Raiders, Ford, Coors. The line is getting longer and longer. Luz is biting her lower lip, punching out another number. A little wet spot appears at the center of one of her boobs, then the other one. I never seen a girl sweat there before. The little baby is still crying, and then I think of something horrible—that's not sweat, it's milk.

"What's your grandma's name?"

"Jeanette." I don't know why I sez Jeanette instead of Rose, it's just the first name that pops into my head.

When that doesn't work, the machine spits out the card. I reach across Luz quick to get it and accidentally brush against her front and feel the cool sticky wetness against my arm. I push through the people waiting in line and make a run for it.

I feel someone hanging on my shirt. "R.D., wait up. Where ya going?" Desiree is jogging beside me, giving me one of her squashed smiles. "Don't be mad at me. Luz just saw some easy money coming. She was gonna give you some of it."

"It was *all* mine."

"It wasn't. You was stealing from your grandpa. You kind of liked the idea, I could tell." She holds my waist and presses her hips against mine. I push her away. "Don't you like me no more, R.D.?"

"Just don't be acting like a ho all the time."

"*You* felt me!" She slaps her hand against one boob. "Member? The day I bought you them fries? You liked me or you wouldn't have done that. Now you've changed. You like that other girl."

"Yeah, right. I got a hundred girls."

"You're mean, R.D. and you stink. You stink like you live in a dump." By now she's screaming, black tears running down her face. People are slowing down, sticking their necks out, looking at us like a car crash.

I walk away. She doesn't follow me, but she keeps yelling all the messed up things I am. She's right about some of them, and I ain't proud of the way I treated her. Trying to go out with someone is like the easiest thing there is to get messed up.

# twenty three

I TAKE ONE STEP into the house and go sniff, sniff, sniff. The place smells so bad it's like something died in here. I don't mean Earl. Funny how you can't smell the place you live in till you go away from it and come back in. I start looking around, not with my own eyes, but the eyes of a visitor, like someone from CPS. There's my dirty plate of spaghetti from the night Earl died, a gray and green web of mold growing over it. There's old cigarette butts and beer bottles and peanut shells. There's even the cigarette butt on the floor I stamped out with my bare foot the night Earl was having an attack. I pick it up and see it's left a brown burn mark in the carpet.

In the kitchen there's an awful stink. The peanut butter and jelly are open on the table from my lunch. I stick my hand in the bread to get a slice and already the first couple of slices are hard from sitting out. I feel the milk jug and it's warm. Oh no! Has a whole jug of milk gone sour just cuz I was too lazy to put it in the fridge? I put everything away. Holding my nose, I go get the moldy spaghetti plate from the living room and wash it. The kitchen still stinks, I don't know why.

I go into my room. It stinks like a locker full of used gym clothes left to rot for a month. My bed stinks, my clothes stink. I pinch the front of my shirt, pull it out from me, and stick my nose inside it. Oh my God, I stink! Then I remember Mr. Walstein touching my shoulder then taking a step back, Miz Silva moving her chair away from me, Desiree screaming, "You stink like you live in the dump." This whole time I been thinking those people were acting like I stink as a person, when really it's my *body* that stinks!

Without Earl telling me to take showers, I been wearing the same clothes three days! I strip everything off me into a heap and take a shower. I dig through my chest of drawers and find a pair of gym shorts that are too short for me and an old T-shirt and put those on. I strip my bed, pick up every last bit of clothing, and drag it all to the back porch. I wish I was paying attention when Earl was trying to teach me how to do laundry. I know you're supposed to separate the whites and darks. First I put in the darks with my jeans on top. I look in the cupboard over the washing machine and see a big white jug of cleaner. I splash an extra dose of that in cuz everything stinks so bad. I fiddle with the knobs till I notice the directions are right on the machine.

I go back to my room and start collecting garbage—soda cans, fast food wrappers, crusts of bread. Then I go for all the little stuff—papers, pencils, crayons, pennies, paper clips. It's easier to dump everything into the wastebasket instead of sorting things out. I pick up a jacket I don't recognize, Silver Boy's snowboarding parka. I don't know why I jacked it, I hardly ever jack stuff. I guess cuz I hate Silver Boy. I hate him for being able to afford good stuff, then just leaving it around like it don't matter.

I find Dominic's literature book and toss it into the wastebasket. It's so heavy it tips the thing over and all my hard work goes spilling out onto the floor. I pick up the book and decide to put it on a shelf instead. Then I think I might've thrown out other good stuff so I turn the wastebasket upside down and start sorting. I find a list of science terms that says across the bottom DO NOT REMOVE FROM YOUR BINDER. Now I know why—cuz it gets thrown out. There's other school papers too. I decide to use those little tab divider things teachers are always yelling about. I print the names of my classes on them, singing a little tune to myself.

I hear the washer go off. I go to the back porch and pull out the whole mess of wet clothes and stuff them in the dryer, thinking this laundry thing is no problem. Then I notice my jeans look messed up, like they're way lighter and splotchy, almost white in places. Maybe they'll get back to normal in the dryer somehow. I switch the dial to hot on the dryer so everything will get dry extra fast, and I load up the washing machine with whites.

I vacuum my room, and since I got going, I vacuum the rest of the house. It makes a kind of tinkling music as all the stuff gets sucked up. Then I notice the toilet is kind of stinky so I scrub it out with Ajax. The dryer buzzes and I dump the clothes out in the basket. I hold up my jeans—man, they're still all splotchy and about two sizes smaller.

The house looks pretty good, but the kitchen still stinks. I follow my nose to the corner, under the table. It's so bad down there it's like a dead animal. I get down on my hands and knees and crawl under the table. It *is* a dead animal. A dead chicken. A chicken that's been plucked and packed and frozen and thawed and is now rotting. A waste of good food. If only I knew how to cook it. I bat it out from under the table with a yardstick, then carry it out to the garbage can. Then I mop the floor where it's been and decide to mop the rest of the kitchen. Dirt and hair and crumbs stick to the mop so now I see why you're supposed to sweep before you mop.

I make three baked potatoes for dinner. I do just what Arnie at the grocery store told me. They smell so good baking my mouth waters. I toss them on a plate, slit them open, and load them with spread and salt. I take a bite. It tastes like dirt. I spit it out, try another bite. It tastes like dirt. I spit it out and slide the whole mess into the garbage.

# twenty four

NONE OF THE NEIGHBORS are out when I back down the drive, but who knows who's at their windows. I got alotta nerve driving in the day, but a rainstorm makes it kind of dark, and I don't know how else I could make it clear over to Jeanette's. I get across town okay, windshield wipers going like crazy. I waste a bunch of time driving around and around the subdivision, looking for Jeanette's street. All the houses are brand new and look about the same. I finally find Jeanette's house on the last corner. I drive by it and park a couple of blocks away.

I walk back, my heart thumping which tells me I'm kind of nervous. When I ring the doorbell I hear quick footsteps and then Jeanette opens the door, her hair still swishing across her shoulders. Her bright smile droops into a scowl.

"What? Ain't I posed to be here? Sunday, one o'clock?"

"It's one-thirty. Our group's been canceled. No one showed up."

"I showed up."

"At least Yeni called. She caught a cold." Jeanette's big, round green eyeballs start swimming, and she drops her head to hide in her hair.

"What about Silver Boy?"

"Silver Boy?"

"Don't Sterling mean silver?"

"You mean *doesn't* Sterling mean silver?" That makes her feel better—correcting my English like a teacher.

She steps over to a little table to get a Kleenex, which gives me a chance to get into the house and shut the door behind me. While she blows her nose I go into a side room. It's like a little fancy living room some houses have that people hardly ever use. Before a puffy flowered sofa is a coffee table all set up with four cloth napkins, teacups, and a huge platter of those lovely Rice Krispie Treats. I can just see Jeanette putting each thing out, imagining how much fun it will be having over her two favorite people—Yeni and Silver Boy.

On a card table is a big piece of cardboard covered in white butcher paper, boxes of sugar cubes, tubes of icing, toothpicks, little flags, knights, and directions to make two castles, a big one and a little one. Jeanette sinks into a folding chair at the card table, but she won't do nothing, not even look at me.

"Are we going to make this dumb castle or what?"

"Show me all the books about castles that you checked out of the library."

I point to the sheets of instructions she must have printed off the internet. "These are better than books. Which one do you wanna make?"

"I knew you wouldn't come through with your part of the assignment."

"Let's just make the damn castle."

She crosses her arms and flips her hair over her shoulders. "I don't associate with boys who throw rocks at me."

"I didn't throw a rock at *you*, I threw it at your case."

"That's the same thing!"

"No, it's not. If I was aiming at you I would've hit you."

"Why would you throw a rock at my trombone?"

"I don't know. Don't you ever do stuff for reasons you don't know?"

"No!" She drops her head, sticks her thumb under the sleeve, and rubs her wrist. She's got on a sweater with stripes of all the colors of the rainbow. She only wears sweaters or tops with long sleeves even when it's hot. "Yes. I guess I do," she sez in a soft, faraway voice.

"I didn't mean to hurt you. I was just mad at you, I guess."

"Why? You hadn't even met me!"

"Cuz you're perfect, okay?"

That gets those green eyeballs bouncing. "You're vindictive! And if you bleach those jeans one more time they're going to rot off you."

"I didn't—oh, my bad. Is that what I done wrong?"

That makes her laugh. She looks over the castle instructions. "The smaller one isn't nearly as impressive."

"You don't gotta always be the best. Let's do the little one."

All of a sudden Jeanette's mom is standing at the doorway trying to slap a smile over a worried face. "I thought I heard voices in here," she sez. Her hair isn't as long, but it's the same honey color as Jeanette's and her eyes are the same green. She has makeup on and a skirt, too dressed up for just hanging around the house. A little fussy baby is squirming on her shoulder.

I remember Miz Silva was mad when I didn't stand up when she came into the room, so I stand up now. "Hi, Miz Whitmore, I'm R.D." She smiles back at me. I'm sure glad I figured out I stunk. I know I must look pretty good in a new Wal-Mart T-shirt and with my jeans shrunk down so there's no saggin-and-baggin. Some kids pay lots of money for jeans already messed up with bleach spots.

"We were trying to decide which castle to make," sez Jeanette. She holds up the plans for the big one. "This one is so awesome."

"Oh my, it is beautiful," sez Miz Whitmore. "But there's just two of you. You don't always have to be the best, honey."

She goes away, and I act real busy breaking open the sugar cube packages. Jeanette measures with a ruler and draws the outline for the little castle.

It's real quiet, except for the baby crying faraway. I try to think of something to say. "How come we're using icing instead of glue? We're not gonna eat it."

"Sugar makes a stronger bond on sugar than glue. Trust

me, I know a lot about chemistry. I want to be an oncologist."

"An on-what?"

"Oncologist. It's a doctor specializing in cancer."

"You think you're gonna find the cure when no one else can?"

"I didn't say that. I'll be treating cancer patients."

I hear a rustling sound and look up. No one's there. Then I hear giggling.

Jeanette is still bent over the sugar cubes. "Marcie and Megan, go away."

Two little blonde girls, about six or so, appear at the door. They nod their heads to a beat only they can hear and begin singing, "Two little lovebirds sitting in a tree. K-I-S-S-I-N-G . . ." They start laughing so hard they can't finish.

"Get out!" Jeanette stamps a foot in their direction, and they run away.

"You're only thirteen and you got your whole life planned out already?" I ask.

"I'm twelve. My birthday isn't until November."

"Whoa, I'll be sixteen in July."

"Sixteen!"

"I could've passed the eighth grade the first time easy, I just didn't do no work."

"You didn't do *any* work. You could correct your grammar if you just think before you speak."

"Yeah? What for? I start talking prep and my homies would jump me."

"Dominic and Gilbert? You really care what they think?"

"Course. Who am I gonna hang out with—Silver Boy?"

"Yeah, who would want to? He's a real tool, isn't he?" She laughs and I'm real glad I cheered her up.

Something tells me there's someone standing at the entryway, even though they don't make a sound. One of the little blonde girls is back. She isn't hiding or giggling like last time, but looking real serious. "Is the castle done yet?"

"No, Maddie," sez Jeanette. "It's going to take a long time. I'll call you when it's done, like I promised."

The little girl walks away.

I lean toward Jeanette and almost whisper, "There's three of them? How can you tell them all apart?"

"Marcie and Megan hang out together and they're brats. Maddie is the good one."

"They leave her out of things? Isn't that sad?"

"No. Marcie and Megan have the same friends and Maddie has her own. Sometimes they all play together, but they're not interested in the same things."

We keep working and pretty soon I can smell something good cooking.

"What do you think your mom is making for dinner?" I ask.

"I don't know. Smells like roast beef."

Now I have a goal in life. It's nothing big like being a cancer doctor. It's eating roast beef!

# twenty five

A WHILE LATER Miz Whitmore brings in hot cocoa and we eat the Rice Krispie Treats. I could eat the whole platter, but I know that's not polite so I just eat half. We get back to building the castle. Every once in a while the triplets come by. I get so I kind of like them, even the bratty ones.

Jeanette stacks sugar cubes faster and faster. I can tell she wants it over with. She's building the fancy parts like the turrets while I do the easy stuff like the drawbridge. I'm starting to get real bored. The baby's cries are getting on my nerves. I shove a sugar cube too hard and a whole row buckles.

"Doesn't that baby ever stop crying?"

"No, he's withdrawing from crack."

I bust out laughing cuz I'm surprised Jeanette has that kind of sense of humor.

"No, really. My mom doesn't think she has enough kids

so my parents take in foster kids. That's how we got Max. We eventually adopted him."

"You think you're gonna adopt the little crackhead?"

She jerks her head up and narrows her eyes. "His name is Shane. He's got grandparents. They'll probably get custody."

"I live with my grandparents. If something happens to them, I become a ward of the county and get sent off to a group home like Selwyn."

"What about a foster family?"

"I'm not a cute little baby. Haven't you noticed? No one wants kids my age, especially boys." I don't know why I'm telling her this. I'm like thinking out loud.

Miz Whitmore comes to the door wearing an apron and an oven mitt. "Hey kids, how much longer? I'm almost ready to put dinner on. When did you tell your parents to pick you up, R.D.?"

"I got to call them. May I use your phone, Miz Whitmore?"

I'm planning on using that old trick of pretending to talk, but Jeanette flips open her cell phone. "What's the number?" When I tell her, she punches it in and hands her phone to me. I just let it ring and ring. If anyone answers, it will be Earl's ghost.

I hand the phone back to her. "My grandpa knows to pick me up here. I'll just wait outside. It's not raining too hard right now, I don't think." I stand and give Miz Whitmore lost puppy dog eyes.

"Oh, you can't wait outside in the rain. Why don't you join us for dinner?"

"Wow! Thanks, Miz Whitmore. Where can I wash up?"

The next thing I know I'm sitting at a long table between Jeanette and a triplet—Maddie, I think, cuz the other two are sitting across from me, side by side. There's also the little guy, Max, in a high chair, but the crack baby ain't in sight and I don't hear it. He must've wore himself out. Miz Whitmore is at one end of the table and Mr. Whitmore is at the other end. There's steaming bowls of broccoli, carrots, baked potatoes, rolls, and a green salad. The fat juicy roast beef sits before Mr. Whitmore, ready to carve.

We all bow our heads and say grace. Jeanette hands me the steaming bowl of broccoli and I start dumping a bunch on my plate. I'm about to plop on the third spoonful when I notice all the triplets and Jeanette are staring at me.

"My bad," I sez. I leave the third spoonful in the bowl.

Miz Whitmore laughs. "It's nice to see a child interested in vegetables."

"I love vegetables! What an awesome dinner, Miz Whitmore."

"Thank you, R.D. It's all easy, nothing fancy at all."

"That's what good cooks say cuz they know what they're doing. Last night I made baked potatoes and they tasted like dirt."

Miz Whitmore blinks. "Did you wash them?"

"Oh! Oh! Is that what you do? My bad!"

"Take a vegetable brush and scrub them really hard, inside all the little eyes."

"What's a vegetable brush?"

"They're little and round and—well, just ask for one at the grocery store."

"I wish I knew how to make those Rice Krispie Treats."

"They're just melted marshmallows and cereal. The recipe is on the box. If you're trying to learn to cook, read the packaging."

The little girls across from me whisper and giggle together. The one with the bigger mouth, Marcie or Megan, I forget which, asks, "Are you Jeanette's boyfriend?"

"Mom!" Jeanette shouts.

"No," I sez, looking straight at them, real cool. "We're just in Miz Trueblood's class together."

"You think she's a good teacher, R.D.?" asks Miz Whitmore. "Jeanette just loves her, but from what she tells us, she can't really control the class."

"She's got lots of good lesson plans," I sez. "And she's good to talk to, like she gives kids extra help if they want it."

"You're the first friend Jeanette has had over," sez Miz Whitmore. "We've just moved from Colorado, you know. It's hard making friends in junior high."

"Jeanette has lots of friends at school," I sez. "She's real popular."

Jeanette smiles big, and I know I've finally said something right so her mom will quit worrying about her.

After dinner everyone gets up and takes their plate to the kitchen, even Max. I say I gotta use the bathroom and as I'm heading through the dark living room, I shout, "Oh, my grandpa's here. Thanks. Bye." I run out the door and down the porch steps.

I think I'm gonna make a smooth getaway, but Miz Whitmore comes out on the porch and yells, "R.D., wait!" She hands me a little round brush with a red handle.

"Whoa, thanks," I sez. I don't know if she's lending it or giving it. I hate it when that happens. I run down the dark, wet street without even trying to explain why there's no car waiting for me. I dash around the corner and jump into the truck.

I'm not so good at turning around so I drive around the whole subdivision looking for the same place I came in. Before long I pass the side of Jeanette's house. There's a light on in an upstairs window and I can hear the sound of a horn blowing out a slow song. I pull over and roll down the window. Light drops of rain splash my face as I sit there listening. The music is low and sad and pours out like honey. Now I get why Jeanette picked the trombone to play.

Driving home, I think of a fun thing to do. I go over to Buzz Aldrin Middle School and pull into the parking space right next to the one marked "Principal." "Hey, Miz Donaldson! Hey, Mr. Bowan!" I yell into the black, wet night. "It's R.D. Mitchell. Look at me! I got my own parking space!"

# twenty six

THE WORST THING about living alone is coming home to an empty house at night. I pull in the drive, turn off the engine, and just stare at the black house. It's so sad and lonely, the corners of the roof seem to sag. The phone begins to ring, a far off *brring-brring*. I take my time climbing out of the truck. There's no rush cuz I know I'll never make it in time.

But when I unlock the door, the phone is still ringing, and I know there's only one person who goes for that many rings. I pick up and sez, "Grandma?"

"Well dammit, it's about time. I've been ringing the damn phone off the wall all the damn day and half the damn week. Where you been? Where's Earl? What the hell's going on?"

"I just got back from my history study group."

"You going to school every day then? Doing your work?"

"I spent the whole day building a castle out of sugar cubes. Reliving history."

"Since when in blazes were castles made out of sugar?" She laughs at her own joke. "Seems like you'd be better off reading a book and writing a report."

"It's learning, Grandma. How's traveling around?"

"It's grand. I met Hairy's whole family. He's got three grown kids, all married, with kids of their own. Would you believe it? They all like me."

"What's not to like about you, Grandma?"

"I've missed being a part of a big family. I don't know what happened to mine. I tried to do right by you and Yolanda, but look where she ended up. In the pen, and before that, a mother at fourteen. You know?"

"I know, Grandma." Yolanda. She don't bring that name up, unless she's been drinking.

"I warned Yolanda about fooling around too young, but she just went wild on me. It wasn't your daddy's fault, neither. Don't ever let her get away with telling you that. He was over there next door, minding his own business. Yolanda was the one with hot pants. You got that?"

"Yeah, Grandma."

"I tried to raise you right. No choice, but to raise you, considering the circumstances. Then what do I do? I go and desert you, my own flesh and blood, so I can go galavanting around the country."

"You didn't desert me. You left me with Earl."

"How is Earl? Does he still hate me?"

"Naw, Grandma. He's over everything, pretty much."

"Is he still coughing a lot?"

"Not near as much."

"That's good. Put him on."

"He ain't here."

"Where is he?"

I sigh, so long and deep I can feel the roast beef in my belly. "I wish I could tell you, Grandma. I just can't." I don't know why that is. Here's my chance to tell my own grandma all my troubles, the only person in all the world who cares a damn about me, and then she could come home and save me from CPS, but I just can't.

"Well, tell him to call me when he gets in."

"Yeah, Grandma."

"You know he won't."

"I know."

"I love ya, boy. It may not seem like it, the way I've left you, but I'll be back visiting soon. You got my numbers now, don't ya?"

When I say I can't find them, she makes me write down Hairy's home phone number and the number of his trucking company.

I hang up, thinking two things: 1. I don't feel so lonely no more; and 2. I never can remember hearing Grandma say the two words, "your daddy."

# twenty seven

MONDAY THE RAIN'S OVER, and it's already heating up. Even at seven in the morning you can tell it's gonna be a hot one, what it usually is during September in the San Joaquin Valley. When I get outside, Dominic and Scraps are already waiting for the bus. Dominic has a blue bandanna tied over his head, which would get him busted if he wore it on school grounds. He pulls a smooth, thin black and silver thing out of his pocket. Scraps leans in to get a better look. Dominic pushes a kind of lever and out pops a blade, nearly sticking Scraps' chest.

"Ah!" Scraps jumps back and Dominic laughs, slicing air.

"Jeez! Where'd you get that?" A real switchblade. I never seen one up close and for reals.

"My uncle Jaime took me out gangbanging Saturday night. He gave it to me."

I've known Dominic long enough to know when he's

lying. Probably he and his mom and brothers were hanging around his uncle's house and he jacked it.

"You better not bring that to school," sez Scraps.

"I gotta have it for protection. Enough dudes know I'm claiming blue. I expect to get jumped any day." He slides the knife shut and drops it in his boot.

Scraps looks down the street. "Bus is late. Maybe you could drive us, R.D." His straight hair swings with his high giggle and he's got Dominic grinning too.

"What? You trippin?"

"We both seen you driving Earl's pickup last night," sez Dominic. "So don't lie."

"Oh yeah, I got my permit, but I can't drive no kids around yet."

"You didn't get no permit," sez Dominic.

"I'm old enough."

"That doesn't mean you got one."

I lean closer to them. "You didn't tell nobody, did you?"

"We don't rat," sez Scraps.

"I had to sneak Earl's truck cuz he was too sick to drive me. He was too out of it to notice, but I ain't gonna risk it again."

"Where'd you go?" asks Scraps.

Somehow I can't tell my homies I was going to some dumb history project, so I sez, "I had to meet someone at the mall."

"Was it that new chick you been hangin with?" asks Dominic. "You get in?"

"Maybe."

"You didn't or you'd say."

"She's a ho. I dumped her."

"You're doing it all wrong," sez Dominic. "First you get in, *then* you got a reason to call her a ho, and then you dump her."

"It ain't worth it, Dom. She's messed up."

Scraps' face is all scrunched up cuz sex worries him. He's Catholic and his church tells him not to do it, not even to his own self.

"I don't wanna make no babies," I sez.

"If a ho gets knocked up it's her own fault. The guy don't have to admit to nothing." He slaps his chest. "My dad never admitted to me."

What can you say to that? My grandma used to say Dominic's mom was no good cuz her three boys have three different fathers and she never married none of them, but I don't care. Flo is always nice to me. Dominic looks a little sad so I smack him in the arm and sez, "Who would want to admit to you?"

He grins and socks me back.

When we get to school, he nods toward the window. "There's your biatch waiting for you."

I glance out the window and see Desiree grinning wide and waving both arms up at me. I slump down in my seat. "God."

"I thought you said you dumped her," sez Dominic.

"I did."

"Did you tell her?"

"Huh . . . I thought I did. Anyways, I said such mean things to her I thought she got it."

"A biatch don't understand mean. You gotta look her right in the eye and say, 'I'm not going out with you no more.'" He jabs the air down with all four fingers.

"Can you do it for me?"

Dominic holds up both palms. "Naw, I ain't getting involved."

I turn to Scraps. "Can you?"

Scraps gets that sick, scrunched-up look. "What if she hits me?"

"Ha! Fraid of a girl! I'll tell her." Dominic looks out the window. "Hey, R.D., she's kind of a hottie. You mind if I hit on her?"

Something stabs my stomach, kind of like a hunger pang. "Why would I care?"

Dominic swipes his bandanna off his head and stuffs it deep in a pocket, then palms his pants to keep them from falling down. He heads off Desiree while I duck into the boys' bathroom. I go inside a stall, yank Silver Boy's jacket out of my backpack, hang it on the hook in there.

When I go outside I see Desiree waving her arms around and yelling, "What do you mean he sez you can have me? I ain't his to give out." Desiree smacks Dominic upside the head. I duck into the auditorium so I don't have to see if Dominic hit her back.

The jazz band is practicing again. There's Jeanette, right up there with the other trombones. It's kind of weird seeing pretty Jeanette with that big metal thing smashed up against her face, kind of like an elephant trunk.

Jazz is like old people's music, but it's not as bad as

regular band music. What they're playing now has a good beat to it—it's some old sixties song. The jazz band is mostly boys. There's only three girls—two on sax and Jeanette on trombone. In jazz band they have solos. A guy stands up in the middle of the song and plays by himself. It's not the regular song, but something made up. Most of them are pretty bad, a couple of off-beat squawks or peeps, then a pause, then a couple more squawks. I keep waiting for Jeanette to show them all up, but she never does stand, none of the girls do. I wonder why.

When the band teacher stops the music and starts talking, I sneak out cuz I don't want Jeanette to think I'm stalking. I liked talking to her at her house but I don't expect her to talk to me at school. I don't think she's stuck-up or too good for me, she's just not in my group and I'm not in hers. That's just the way things are.

# twenty eight

I GOT DETENTION after school cuz I was truant last week, the day Earl died. It seems like Earl's been gone a long time, but I ain't even made it through four days. I don't feel like going to detention, so I start walking to the bus. If you miss a detention they give you two more. Last year school ran out before I finished all my detentions, but they wipe your slate clean when the new school year begins. Right now I only got two to do, which seems like hardly nothing. Then I remember Mr. Bowan calls home if you miss a detention, so I turn around and head back for the detention classroom.

It's real quiet in there. The detention lady Miz Valdez checks me in and assigns me a seat somewheres in the middle of the classroom. She don't give us no special work to do. Most kids just stare at the wall.

"R.D., R.D.! *Psst!*"

I look up and see it's Desiree sitting in the first desk, first row. I been hiding out from her all day, which is easy cuz we don't got no classes together. I don't pay no attention to her. I get out my binder and start working on my algebra homework. I almost got the first problem when a note drops in my lap, all folded up fancy in a neat triangle packet. I open it up.

hey homie wassup mah man me notta lot jes chilli
wheR U ben hangin all day I ben looking 4 U
im soRRy U had 2 leav the mall so soon im soRRy
we fot it all my falt R.D.
I couldnt sleep laz nite woRin about it baby
I still luv U lotz R.D. Domnick tole me you dont
  wanna go out W/Me but
I still wanna go out W/U. I didn't mean 2B
  jeloz UR jes so hot other
chickas look at UR hot bod I cant help it I git
  so jelloz I no U like me 4 realZ
UR jes mad at Luz for jacking your gramps
  ATM card UR mine R.D. it
waz ment 2B
w/b
bye
luv alwayz
UR blatch Desiree

Jeez. I stuff the note in my pocket and get back to work. Before long, another note hits me in the face. I don't read it, just stuff it.

After a while I hear Miz Valdez say, "I'll take that." I look up and Desiree is about to hurl another note. She stretches her arm down and sez, "No."

Miz Valdez just stands there with her hand out.

Desiree pops the folded paper in her mouth and the kids laugh.

Miz Valdez moves her open palm under Desiree's mouth. "I'll take that."

There's so much paper in Desiree's mouth she starts to drool. Finally she's gotta spit the note out in Miz Valdez's hand.

"Yew, sick," sez someone. "HIV."

Miz Valdez don't worry about HIV, she's tough like that. I've seen her peel gum off textbooks and suckers off the carpet. She tosses Desiree's note in the wastebasket, no big deal. If Desiree hadn't slimed it she probably would've read it.

When detention gets out, I walk real fast out of there, my legs swishing like scissors. I hear Desiree calling, "R.D., R.D.," but I run into the boys' bathroom. I'm acting real chicken, but there's just no saying no to Desiree.

I wait about fifteen minutes, and when I get out of the bathroom there's not a kid around. I might've even missed the late bus. As I'm running to the loading zone I look down a hall and see a blonde girl sitting on the sidewalk, dressed in gym clothes for volleyball practice. It's Jeanette and she's not just sitting, her legs are sticking out all funny. When I get closer I see her stuff is scattered all over.

"Jeanette! You okay?"

She looks up, sees it's me. "Go away. Leave me alone."

"What happened? Did you trip?"

"I hate this school. I want to move back to Colorado."

Her trombone case is thrown open and all the pieces dumped out. Her backpack is torn apart, the rings of her binder pulled open. I run around the strip of lawn between buildings, trying to catch all her loose papers blowing away. I hand them to her, but she won't take them.

"You get jumped?"

She looks at the papers and moans, "My science is crinkled."

I try to flatten the top paper out, but rip it on accident. I stuff all the papers in the binder and zip it up. "Seems like it had to be more than just one dude to do all this damage."

"I think it was just one. A girl." She wipes her eyes and sniffles. She begins patting around her, peeking into all the pockets of her backpack.

"What did she look like?"

Jeanette shakes her head. "She attacked me from behind. She was screaming threats at me. She was all, 'Stay away from my man or I'll frickin kill you, I'll frickin pull out all your blonde hair.'"

"*After* she kills you?"

"She's crazy. She pulled me down by the hair." Jeanette rubs her scalp.

"Maybe she got you mixed up with someone else. Were you all by yourself?"

"Sort of. I was walking to the front of the school with Yeni and Donna and then I realized I'd dropped my favorite pen, so I retraced my steps, looking down and—*pow!* Yeni and Donna heard me screaming, but by the time they got to me, she was gone. They've gone to the office for help."

"You gotta favorite pen?"

"My cell phone is missing. I have to call my mom."

Some jazz tune starts up, far away. It's hard to tell where it's coming from at first. We both look up at the roof.

"I'll get it." I try to shimmy up a pole and grab the roof, but slide right down, scraping my hand. It's embarrassing.

"Never mind. Donna and Yeni went for help."

I want to be the hero in this, I don't know why. I run around the building, remembering how Scraps and I got up on the roof the day he skated off it. I climb on a low pillar, scramble up two tree limbs, leap onto a wall around a storage area, and crawl onto the roof. I'm running across it when the jazz music starts up again.

"I got it," I yell down to Jeanette.

"Don't answer it!"

I flip it open and sez, "Hello?"

"Oh! I think I've got the wrong number."

"Oh hi, Miz Whitmore. It's R.D."

"I told you not to," Jeanette yells up to me. She's on her feet now, brushing herself off.

"Why are you answering Jeanette's phone?" ask Miz Whitmore.

"She was busy a minute. Here she is." I start to swing it before the toss.

"Don't throw it!" Jeanette yells up.

"Oh, Miz Whitmore, thanks for the roast beef dinner."

"You're welcome, R.D. I'm glad you enjoyed it."

"And the Rice Krispie Treats. Did you get that little crack baby to shut up?"

"Shane is resting more peacefully today, thank you. I'd love to chat, but I need to arrange Jeanette's transportation."

"Can she call you right back? In just a sec, okay?" I snap the phone shut before she can answer. I crawl to the edge of the roof, lay on my belly, hang my arm over the edge, and toss.

Jeanette kind of fumbles it, but manages to grab it against her body. She scowls up at me and sez, "I told you not to throw it."

"I told you not to throw it," I sez back. Some thanks I get for all I done for her.

She calls her mom and sez, "Nothing's wrong. No, really."

Next I see the tops of Yeni's and Donna's and Mr. Bowan's heads. I crawl backward till I'm out of sight, then scramble down the way I come up. As I cross the street to the City Coach stop I keep looking over my shoulder, watching my back. Where did Desiree disappear to so fast?

# twenty nine

THURSDAY I RUN OUT OF POTATOES. I'm not worried though, it's easy to scrounge 99¢ around the house so I can buy another whole ten pounds. I tear the cushions off the sofa and shove my hand down the back. I come up with peanut shells, lint balls, a comb, and twenty-seven cents. I tip the easy chair over. *Tinkle, tinkle.* Another seven cents. The junk drawer on the back porch is the best. I dig through my old lunch cards, receipts, washers, pee-wee golf pencils, and come up with fourteen pennies, one nickel, and two quarters. Potatoes, come to Papa!

I head down the hall into Earl's room cuz I still keep the keys to the truck in the little green saucer on his chest of drawers. As soon as I step into Earl's room, the phone rings, ripping through the quiet. I run the hell out of there. His room still makes me jumpy. I remember it was one week ago today that he died. I stand frozen in the hall, waiting for the phone to stop ringing.

I don't bother answering it cuz it's probably just some guy wanting his oil changed, and I'm tired of lying about Earl being too sick to work on cars. I got to go get the keys, but now I'm a little afraid to go back into Earl's room. I feel him in other parts of the house, in the yard, the garage, even in the truck, but it's in his room where his ghost is the strongest. I get up my courage, but as soon as I step foot into his room I get a creepy feeling. I tiptoe to the chest of drawers and reach out.

"I'll be real careful, Earl," I sez out loud. I grab the keys and run.

When the phone starts up again, I answer it. "Yeah?"

"Is that any way to answer the phone, scumbag?"

"Oh, hi Bobby. Earl ain't here."

"I've been calling all week, I've been by about five times. The place is like a ghost town. Sometimes the truck is there, sometimes it isn't. What's up?"

"Earl's in the hospital," I blurt out real fast. It's easy to lie to Bobby cuz he's so dumb.

"The hospital! How come no one told me? What for? How's he doing?"

"Better now. He was having trouble breathing."

"Who's looking after you?"

"Grandma's here," I sez, thinking that ought to keep him from snooping around. Bobby hates Grandma.

"Rose is back?" He chuckles in a mean way. "What happened to her hairless Romeo?"

"I told her Earl was bad off and she come back to take care of us."

"Real noble. Put her on."

"She ain't here right now."

"Damn you, you little bugger, you better not be lying to me. You better not be living there on your own, and you sure as hell better not be driving that truck."

I slam the phone down. In three seconds it starts ringing again. I walk down the hall and set the truck keys back in the green saucer. When I head out the back door, the phone is still ringing.

It's a mile walk to Wong's Market and it's hot—Indian summer, they call it. It means it don't start cooling off till October. By the time I get to the store, I'm all sweaty. The air conditioning hits me smack in the face. I boogie over to the pile of ten-pound sacks of potatoes. I'm about to heave a sack off the counter, when I stop, my hands pressing against the hard lumps of potatoes. The sign doesn't say 99¢ no more, it sez $1.99.

"Can I help you?"

It's the same Arnie guy that helped me before. "How could the price go up so much? They were just a dollar last week."

"Last week they were on sale. This week it's onions. Hey, I remember you. How did your baked potatoes turn out?"

"You didn't tell me I had to wash them."

He laughs and I have to laugh too. He swings his forefinger out, thumb up, like drawing a gun on me. "But you figured it out."

"Yeah. Then they were good." I look behind him at the onions. I don't think I could eat a whole plate of onions, even if I did know how to cook them. I start walking away empty-handed.

Arnie yells after me. "Hey, what about your potatoes?"

I jingle the change in my jeans pocket. "I only got a dollar."

"Oh, yeah? Hey, come back."

I take a step forward, he takes a step forward. All of a sudden we're standing closer together than people usually do. I can see pimples underneath his black scruffy beard.

He looks around, lowers his voice. "I can get you your potatoes, but you're going to have to work for them. Come back to the store later on, say about ten. Around the back."

I know something ain't right. "You can hire people?" I ask. My tone of voice sez I know he can't and his black eyes cut into me like I dissed him.

"I can get you your potatoes," he sez again. He smiles then, but it isn't a nice smile like he give me just a minute ago when I was a customer, now it's a mean smile people give when they know they got you.

Walking home, listening to my stomach growl, I'm looking into people's yards for food. Why didn't I think of it before? There's food growing all around me. Lots of oranges and grapefruits, but they're not ripe yet. I see peach trees, apricots, nectarines, plums, but it's too late for them. What's left is under the trees, rotted and bird-pecked. I look between the slats of a fence and see a vegetable garden. It's got tomatoes, bell peppers, and big long zucchinis.

The house is still like nobody's home or maybe they're eating dinner. It's getting dark. I make little scratching sounds on the fence and wait. There's no dog. I climb the fence and grab a tomato, then another, using my shirt for a basket. I pick a yellow squash, a big ole zucchini. I stumble over a monster watermelon. That's better than anything, but I know I can't climb the fence with it and if I tossed it over it would get wasted on the sidewalk.

I hear a sliding glass door open and look over to the house. Someone's standing on the patio in the dusk. His straight arm rises up in front of him. Jeez, it's a gun! This guy is gonna kill me for a couple of tomatoes?

I drop the zucchini and run. One foot is on the fence and a knee is on the top railing when I hear rat-a-tat-tat against the wood. Something hits my butt—*yow!* It's only a BB, but it stings like hell. I'm over the fence and hit the sidewalk running. I'm nearly home when I slow down, gasping, my side aching. One of the tomatoes is smashed against my T-shirt. I eat it anyways, scrape the little yellow seeds off with my teeth. It's yummy, as sweet as fruit. No store sells a tomato this good.

I'm not sure what to do with the yellow squash. I wash it and stick it in a 400 degree oven like a potato. Then I think of something. I get a bowl, go outside to the fence, reach up, and pick bunches of purple grapes. Old Man Luna is the one growing them, but they're hanging in my yard so no one can say I'm stealing them. Some of them are sour and all of them got gritty little seeds I gotta spit out, but some of them are real good.

I go into the kitchen to check out the squash. It's oozing juice which sizzles and burns at the bottom of the oven. I take it out and smash it with spread. It's good. Then I remember Miz Whitmore said directions are on packages. I go into the pantry and get the half bag of elbow macaronies. It sez to put four quarts of water in a large saucepan and bring it to a rolling boil for ten minutes. I don't know how much four quarts is and I don't know what a rolling boil is, so I just put some water in a pot and put it on the stove. It takes a long time for little bubbles to get in the water. I remember the saying, "It's as easy as boiling water," but things are only easy if you know how to do them.

The macaronies and water start boiling too much. Now I know what a rolling boil is, cuz the water and macaronies roll right over the sides of the pot. Little macaronies are swimming all over the place. I try to scoop some back into the pot. When the ten minutes are up, I'm supposed to drain well. I know what a drain in the sink is, but I don't know what drain means in cooking. I skip that part, take the pot over to the sink, and with a big fat spoon, hold the macaronies in the pot and pour all the water out.

I dump the macaronies on a plate, put spread on top, salt it, and stir it up. Someday, when I get really rich, I'm going to buy myself a block of cheese.

# thirty

"I GOT TO TAKE THE TRUCK, Earl," I sez. "It's late and I'll be coming home even later. I could get jumped in this hood." I'm walking down the hall, talking to Earl and thinking to myself it would be easier to keep the keys to the truck in my room instead of the green saucer on the chest of drawers in Earl's room. But I think I'm supposed to argue with Earl's ghost every time I take the truck.

I drive over to Wong's and park in the dark empty lot a far ways from the store. I go around the back and find Arnie. There's a big bunch of boxes of produce on the dock. He shows me how to load four boxes on a dolly, then wheel them into the store and unload them in a back room. He helps me with the first couple of loads, but then his cell phone rings.

He stands around talking while I load up the dolly again. When I go inside the store, I can see through the open swinging door that there's another guy stocking shelves. He's nodding his head and kind of dancing around to music I can't hear. Then I notice the earphones and the wire worming down into his clothes. He don't see me, which is a good thing, cuz maybe Arnie isn't supposed to have me here helping him.

When I go out to the dock, Arnie is making another call, getting a poker game together. After I make another three trips with the dolly, a couple of guys show up.

"Hey Arnie, I see you got some help tonight," sez one fat dude.

Arnie lights a cigarette and blows smoke. "Yep. I got me a hired hand."

The other two guys laugh. They all sit on crates and Arnie pulls out a deck of cards while I lift a real heavy crate of oranges. My back is starting to ache. My butt feels like it's kind of bruised. I rub it and remember the BB.

I keep loading up the dolly while Arnie keeps winning the pot. I count the chimes of St. Joseph's sounding off in the distance—twelve. Soon after that, Arnie's card-playing friends leave, and he helps me stack the last load of boxes. I push them into the back room while Arnie stands on the dock counting his money. I walk back out to the dock, so tired it's like I'm sleeping on my feet.

He slaps me on the back. "Good job, kid. You're a born worker. Wait here." He goes into the store and comes back with a ten-pound bag of potatoes. "Here ya go."

I almost forgot what I was working for. "Hey, that's not right."

He thinks it's real funny. "What do ya mean? I asked you

to do a little work for me and told you I'd give you a sack of potatoes for it. A deal's a deal, right?"

"The store is paying you, but you stoled from the store to pay me."

"What do you care? The store expects a little pilfering—it's human nature."

"You owe me, not the store."

"Okay." He takes the potatoes out of my arms, sets them down, takes out his wallet, thick with all the money he's won from the poker game, and counts out some money. It seems like it's a lot, but when he hands it to me, I see it's all ones, five of them. Five bucks is a lot of money to me, but I'm sure the store is paying him way more for the work I did.

I start to walk away, and then I realize I don't have what I've come for. The store is closed and I can't drive the truck over in broad daylight to shop tomorrow. He's got me.

"Wait a minute. I changed my mind. Here." I hand him back the money and take back the potatoes. I just can't stand that mean smile he has. "You're a cheat," I sez, and start to walk off.

"Hey man, don't go away mad." He keeps on laughing at me. "I'll get you a few more things. I'll even put money in the till."

I know he's lying, but now I don't even care. "Okay. Some Rice Krispies and some marshmallows. Some broccoli and some macaronies." I don't dare ask for a block of cheese—it costs too much.

He goes into the store and I have to wait a long time. I wonder if he ditched me somehow. I'm about to go in after him. I hope the stock boy sees me and Arnie gets in trouble. Just then, he comes out with a big sack of groceries. It makes me feel a whole lot better.

I walk out to the truck, throw the bag in the passenger's seat and climb in. I start up, put it in gear, and start rolling forward. I'm also looking in the bag. Arnie got me everything I wanted, but the macaroni is different. Instead of a plain bag, he put in three boxes of macaroni and cheese.

*Crash!* There's a ugly scraping metal sound. I lurch forward and bump my nose on the steering wheel. *Yow!* Holding my nose, which starts to drip blood, I jump out to see what I hit. It's one of those big concrete pillars that holds up the light poles. There's a big dent on the driver's side, the left headlight is smashed in. Oh no, oh no! Jeez, Earl, I'm sorry.

I get back in the truck and throw it in reverse. There's some more awful scraping before I get the truck free. I hightail it out of there before Arnie can come around the store and laugh at me some more.

# thirty one

*EARL DIDN'T GET NO FUNERAL!* It's the first thing I think Saturday morning. It wakes me up and makes me sit right up in bed. I take an extra long shower, and plan the whole thing out. After I dry myself, I hang the towel on the rack. It ain't hard once you get used to it. What's harder is standing dripping wet in the shower, reaching around, and finding your towel is a cold soggy lump on the floor.

I dig deep into my closet and come up with a long-sleeved white shirt. Grandma bought it for me a couple of years ago. The cuffs hit me about halfway to my elbows and I can't button the top two buttons over my chest. I put on my bleach-spotted jeans and notice the threads are showing where the bleach ate through.

After a breakfast of dry Rice Krispies, I gather my supplies for the funeral, and go out into the backyard to pick the perfect spot. I head straight for Earl's rosebushes. The grass is higher than my ankles. We don't have much of a lawn no more cuz of the car parts and other junk, but I still gotta figure out how to mow it one of these days. The roses are still in bloom. There's pink ones, white ones, yellow ones, red ones, and some colors in between. There's lots of weeds too, nearly as tall as the bushes. I know how to weed, that's one thing Grandma made me do.

I set my things on the sidewalk, get down on my knees, and start pulling weeds. The ground is still soft from all the rain, so it's pretty easy to do. I make a long rectangle of bare dirt next to the roses. It sort of looks like a grave, but I know it's too narrow for a real one. I smooth the dirt out, wash my hands with the hose, and wipe them on an old rag. Next I find a slab of concrete from Earl's junk heap and drag it over as a kind of gravestone. On top of that I put the American flag folded in a tight triangle. Next to the flag, I set Earl's Vietnam vet cap. It all looks so official, I imagine I'm in a real cemetery, at a real grave, at a real funeral.

I stand straight and tall and say, "We are gathered here . . ." The sound of my own voice creeps me out. If the neighbors heard me, they'd think I'm nuts. And there's no we here, it's just me. I start over in a whisper. "Here lies Earl Mitchell, a man who . . ." That ain't right either.

"Here lies the *spirit* of Earl Mitchell. He was loved by R.D. Mitchell and Rose Mitchell and Nadine Coombs and Bobby Scudder. He proudly served his country in the Vietnam War and all he got back was Agent Orange that killed him and a little bit of money. He was a good man. He was good with his hands. He knew alot about helicopters and cars and he loved the Raiders and he let me back cars down the driveway sometimes. He took me fishing once and camping once too, only we couldn't really stay overnight cuz we forgot the sleeping bags, but we cooked hot dogs on sticks with the tall sequoia trees all around us and it was all right. Earl never left me like Yolanda and Grandma."

I get kind of choked up then and have to stop a minute. I never thought about any of this stuff, but it's right. "I'm gonna really miss you, Earl," I sez, not talking *about* Earl no more, but talking *to* him like he can hear me. "I really don't know what I'm gonna do without you, but I'm trying to get along. I really do need you to take care of me cuz no one else will, and I'm about to be sent to the home any day now. I'm sorry you didn't live to see me make you proud. I don't know how I could ever do that, but if you were still alive, I'd sure try. Even though you're dead I still feel you here with me, Earl, and I guess that's a good thing even though it creeps me out sometimes, especially at night in the dark when I'm doing something I'm not supposed to like taking the truck. Well, that's about all I got to say, but I know people are supposed to read stuff at funerals cuz I seen it in movies, and I found something good."

I pick up Dominic's literature book and turn it to the place I got marked. It's a poem called, "O Captain, My Captain." I know Walt Whitman wrote it when Abraham Lincoln got shot. Course I never thought of Earl as being my captain, but when I was in the shower making plans, this was the first thing I thought of. I begin to read.

> *O Captain! my Captain! our fearful trip is done;*
> *The ship has weather'd every rack, the prize we*
> *sought is won;*

When I get to my favorite part, my voice rises up to nearly a shout and I get a little shake in my voice and beat my chest three times.

*But O heart! heart! heart!*
*O the bleeding drops of red,*
*Where on the deck my Captain lies,*
*Fallen cold and dead.*

I'm so carried away that at first I don't notice another voice rising up with mine, shouting, "Doesn't anyone around here have enough sense to take in the mail?"

I turn and see Bobby standing right beside me, his fat hairy gut peeking out from under his shirt. His arms are loaded down with all sorts of junk mail and envelopes that he dumps on Dominic's literature book. "Here. The box was so overflowing that knothead mailman couldn't even shut it."

"Oh jeez, thanks, Bobby. I guess I—uh, we—forgot all about it." I'm real embarrassed about Bobby catching me in the middle of Earl's funeral. I wonder how much of it he heard. Has he caught on that Earl is dead?

He looks down at the rectangle I've cleared of weeds. "For crying out loud, you moron! Don't you know it's against the law for our flag to touch the ground?"

"No."

"Well it is, you idiot. I could have you arrested right now. I could make a citizen's arrest." He picks up the flag and brushes the dirt off. "What the hell happened to the truck?"

I look down at the ground and mumble, "Nothin."

"Don't tell me nothing. The whole driver's side is bashed in, headlight gone and everything."

"Grandma don't see too good at night no more. She was at the store. Hit something pulling out of the parking lot, a light pole I think."

"Was she drinking? I better have a talk with her." He heads toward the house.

"Hold on. Wait." I chase after him, but it ain't easy with the mail sliding all over the open literature book. But my legs are longer than Bobby's and I manage to rush ahead of him and stand between him and the back door. He tries to reach around me for the knob, but I block his hand with my hip. "She ain't here. She's visiting Earl at the hospital."

"That's another lie you told me. Like a fool I went over there to visit him and they had no record of him ever being in there."

"You went to Kaweah Delta Hospital? He never was in there. He's at the Veterans' Hospital."

"In Palo Alto? How the hell did Rose get all the way up there?"

"She took the train."

"You lying brat! The train doesn't go from here to there."

"She took the bus, then the train."

"How many days is Rose gonna be up there? She better not have left you alone, that's just asking for trouble."

He's got me real scared now, but I act cool. I sez, real bored-like, "Don't have a cow. She left early this morning and she's coming back tonight. You can call her later if you don't believe me."

"Yeah?"

"Yeah."

"Maybe I better have a look around inside anyway. Maybe I ought to take the keys to the truck, just for safe-keeping until Rose gets back." He tries to elbow me away from the door, but I stand my ground. An envelope slides off the top of the mail and drops to the steps.

With a grunt, Bobby stoops over and picks it up. "Hey, this is Earl's Marine pension check. He must be real bad off not to be watching the mail for this." He holds the envelope up close to his face, bends it a little, and tries to peak inside the little hole where the address is. "Maybe I better find a way to get it into the bank for him."

"My grandma can do it."

"Okay, but don't forget to tell her about it. I'll just set it on his desk." He tries to wiggle around me again.

"I'll put it on Earl's desk. Grandma said I couldn't let nobody in the house."

"She didn't mean me."

"She meant especially you. She said, 'Don't let that creep Bobby Scudder come snooping round here. He'll be after Earl's pension check for sure.' I saw you trying to look in the envelope and I'm telling Grandma."

"Why, you little jerk." He throws it against my chest. He takes a step back and glares at me. "There's something fishy around here."

I sniff the air. "More like garlicky. Oh! It's your stinking salami breath. Why don't you leave and stop stinking up our yard?"

Maybe I shouldn't have said 'yard,' cuz he starts looking around again. He walks slowly over to the rosebushes, stares at the dirt rectangle awhile, then turns to leave.

He opens the gate and sez again, "Something's fishy and I'm going to find out what it is."

When I hear his Pontiac's wheels skid out of the drive, I breathe out loud and long. I realize I been holding my breath since he left the yard.

# thirty two

IT SURE WAS DUMB not getting the mail but I forgot all about it. My eyes catch the words 'United States Marines.' When I get inside, I rip open the envelope and find a check for a few hundred bucks. I'd be rich if I could cash it. I sit at the kitchen table and sort the rest of the mail, putting the ads in one pile and the envelopes in another. The envelopes are all bills: gas, water, medical clinic, phone, and one from Sears with a set of tires on it. There's Earl's disability check from Social Security too, bigger than his pension.

I know where Earl's bank is, a long ways from here, on the other side of town. I could go down there and just ask them if I could put these two checks in for Earl. If I say he's too sick to do it for himself, would they let me? Somebody's got to look after Earl's affairs now that he's gone. Sometimes Dominic's mom don't have the money to pay the bills and they get stuff shut off, like the electricity and phone. First I gotta get these checks in the bank, then I gotta find a way to pay these bills. No store would take a check I wrote, but why wouldn't these companies? How would they know it was me writing the checks if I just mailed them in?

I go to Earl's rolltop desk. In one of the little pigeonholes is his checkbook and in another one is a thick envelope from the bank with all the checks he wrote last month. I take this stuff back to the kitchen table. I get out some binder paper and start practicing Earl's shaky ole signature. I know what I'm doing is against the law—it's forgery. People trying to use it on other people's checks always get caught and go to jail. It's called "passing bad checks." But I'm just gonna pay Earl's bills with Earl's money. What's wrong with that?

I add up the two checks, then I add up all the bills. Then I subtract the total amount of the bills from the total of the checks. Luckily I don't get negative numbers. I thought negative numbers were totally useless, but now I see that a negative number would mean Earl don't have enough money to cover these bills. I come out ahead a couple of hundred dollars. Then I remember I seen another bill on Earl's desk. I go get it. It's the electric bill—$263.08. Wow! I know it's high cuz of the air conditioner running in the summer.

I subtract the electricity bill, which leaves $47.36. I get real sad then. Earl was poor, poorer than I ever knew. He always said he fixed cars for something to do. Now I know he really needed the money.

I sit there for what seems like hours, writing out checks to pay the bills. There's stuff to do on the bills and each one is a little different. You got to write in a little box how much money you're sending and you got to tear a little part off and keep a little part for yourself. Most companies want all the money you owe them, but Sears just wants ten bucks instead of the whole two hundred. If people only pay ten dollars a month and buy two hundred dollars' worth of stuff a month, how do they ever catch up?

I decide I been working pretty hard and deserve a treat. I get out a long cake pan. I'm supposed to put cooking spray in it, but I don't got none so I skip it. I put a big pot on the stove, measure out the spread, count out forty marshmallows. I can't resist popping one into my mouth. Then I pop another one and another one and the only way I can stop eating marshmallows is by putting a twist tie on the bag while I have one in my mouth.

I stir and stir. The heat is making me sweat and my hand is getting a cramp. When the marshmallow stuff is all creamy, I take the pot off the stove and add the Rice Krispies. There's supposed to be six cups, but I've been eating them, so I only got three and part of a cup. I dump them in and stir them around and when everything looks pretty well mixed, I dump it in the cake pan.

Rice Krispie marshmallow stuff sticks to the pot, the spoon, my fingers. It sticks everywhere but in the cake pan. I even get some in my hair. Then the doorbell rings. I start licking my fingers real fast, but I can't get cleaned up enough to turn the knob before the person at the door will get tired of waiting and walk away.

It couldn't be nobody good anyways. Probably Officer Hackett checking up on me or CPS or Bobby back again to cause more trouble. I decide to just pretend that nobody's home. I lick the big stirring spoon and duck my head into the pot to lick it and then I hear something. I look up real quick and see Dominic standing in the kitchen sink window, grinning at me like out of a picture frame.

"Hey foo, how come you don't answer the door?"

I hold up the pot and try to talk around the gob stuck to the roof of my mouth. "I'm in a sticky situation."

"Yeah? Sure alotta stuff messed up round here." He swipes his blue bandanna off his head, wraps it around his hand, and begins pulling shards of glass out of the window frame. He bounds through the window, not summersaulting into the sink like I did, but landing on his feet like a cat. He palms his jeans up, alotta his boxers showing over the top of them.

"Hey, what's this?" He sits at the table, reaches into the cake pan, and stuffs a fistful of treat into his mouth. I dig in too. We don't say nothing for awhile, just munch and munch with the late afternoon sun streaming yellow into the kitchen, making it all warm and friendly, and for once I'm glad Earl's not around cuz he would've kicked Dominic out.

"Good, huh?"

"It's alright. How'd you smash up the truck?"

"Over at Wong's. At night. Hit one of them cement things."

"I knew something like that would happen with no driver's training."

"I can drive fine. I just wasn't looking where I was going."

Dominic tilts his head back and laughs. I can see white marshmallow stuff in his mouth, and I gotta laugh too. He gets bored just eating and starts tossing up gobs of marshmallow, trying to get it to stick to the ceiling. When he finally does, he laughs harder. I'm getting pist off cuz he's wasting my good food and I know who's gotta clean up after him.

"Stop! Earl will hear you and then he'll kick you out."

"Earl is gonna hear me?"

"Yeah. He's asleep in his room. He's real sick these days, ya know. Hardly ever gets out of bed."

Dominic doesn't believe me for a minute, but I act like I don't notice. He gets up, opens the fridge. "Got anything to drink?"

"There's milk." I get two glasses out of the cupboard.

He bends down and starts moving things around on the bottom shelf. "Earl's a drunk, ain't he? A drunk always has beer around."

"Sit down." I shove him out of the way, too hard, so he stumbles backward and falls into his chair.

"I am sitting down," he sez, and we laugh some more.

I pour us glasses of milk. It goes down cool and creamy, the perfect thing to wash the marshmallow out of our mouths.

Dominic notices the pile of paid bills with the checkbook on top and slides it in front of him. "What's this?"

"Nothin. Earl just got done paying the bills."

"Thought you said he don't get outta bed."

"Well, he's got to sometimes. Drink up. We can go play some games."

Dominic looks at me with bouncing eyes. "Just so long as Earl don't hear us." He takes the two checks out of the checkbook and looks them over. "Too bad we can't find a way to cash these. We could have some hecka fun."

"Right." I slide the checks out of his hand, stick them

back in the checkbook, restack the bills, and shove the pile out of his reach. "Come on."

I lead him into my room. He sprawls on the bed and picks up my Xbox. I stand at the doorway, my head cocked, like I'm listening to something. "Hold up. I think I hear Earl."

He smirks at me. "I didn't hear nothin."

"That's cuz he was calling me when you was talking. I'm gonna go check on him."

"You do that," sez Dominic, already starting the first game without me. "You go check on Earl."

I tiptoe down the hall, open the door to Earl's room. It's dark and kinda smelly like old, trapped air. I stare at his sagging bed, imagining him in it. Then I tiptoe out. I go back into my room, but Dominic's not there. He's not in the bathroom either. I find him in the living room, pawing through the pigeonholes of Earl's rolltop desk.

He looks up when he sees me. "Got any smokes?"

"You know Earl hides his cigarettes."

"Yeah. Hey foo, I gotta book."

I haven't had much company lately and I'm disappointed he's going away so soon. "I thought we was gonna play some games."

"Ah, I better get home. My uncle Jaime is coming over for dinner."

"Well then, later." I raise my hand up to slap palms, but something stops me. It's his eyes—hard and flat.

Dominic heads out the back door and I look around the kitchen. Right away I know there's something different about it, but I don't see what. I stare at the pile of paid bills and the two checks on the table. I feel prickles at the back of my neck like the hair is rising up there.

I tear through the house, fling open the front door and don't even take time to shut it. I leap off the porch, cross the street. Sprinting down the sidewalk, I make some chickens flutter their wings. I barrel past a Hmong grandpa and his pregnant daughter, watching their faces grow wide with fear. I'm closing in on Dominic. He's easy to catch with his slow, wide-kneed strut. He hears me coming, but too late. I clamp down on his shoulder and whirl him around.

"Give it."

"What?" His chin is raised, his steely eyes reflect the pride and the pain of the falsely accused. I seen him give that look to teachers a hundred times and it makes me crazy that he's using it on me.

I sock him in the gut. He doubles over and I grab the back of his neck, dash him to the ground, and start throwing punches. He comes to life then and starts fighting back. We roll over and over into the street so that if a car came by we'd both be road kill. I ain't fought him for reals since the third grade when he took my first Gameboy for a swim. I've always been bigger than him, but now I'm even bigger. I'm beating the crap out of him. I'm so mad I could kill him. Blood is running out of his nose and drool is dripping out of his mouth and big ole tears start spurting out of his eyes.

That's what makes me stop hitting and start realizing his way of thinking. Dominic and Earl have been enemies from the start, and Dominic would never stop to think that ripping him off is the same as ripping me off. Maybe he thinks a dead man don't need to write checks. I'm sitting on top of him, pinning his wrists to the ground and we're both panting and heaving.

He grunts. "Get offa me, foo."

I let go of his wrists to pat his front pockets. He socks me a good one on the side of my head, but I'm beyond feeling physical pain. I move off of him, roll him over, and pat his back pockets. I feel the checkbook in his left pocket and slide it out. Then I let him up.

We stand there together, brushing our clothes off, pressing our ribs, our arms, our faces, checking for damage. Neither of us is hurt much.

"What'd you go and jump me for, R.D.? I was just playing with ya."

All these years I've been thinking old Earl was too hard on Dominic. Now I realize he was right about him all along. "Earl don't allow you in our house, member? Stay out."

"I was gonna give it back. For reals." He punches me lightly on the arm, which is kinda bruised from him punching me hard. "I was just waitin for you to notice it was gone."

"You lie."

"It's cool, dude. I see how it is." His chin tilts up and his eyes go flat. He turns slowly, raises his shoulders to his ears, and starts strutting home like I'm the one that done him wrong.

I get mad all over again. He's getting off too easy. I charge after him, reach out, grab two handfuls of denim on either side of him and yank his pants down. He reacts, but too late. Raising a knee to run, he trips, falls facedown on the sidewalk. He couldn't get me back if he tried, his feet all tangled up in his monster pants, so he just starts laughing.

"You turd," I sez. Finally I start laughing too.

# thirty three

MONDAY AFTER SCHOOL I jump on the *sur* bus instead of my own to get over to Earl's bank. Inside the bank is a line and I get into it. I take out Earl's checkbook and the two checks that I been keeping in his wallet. As I'm waiting my turn, two little wet dots show up on the checks where my fingertips are. Jeez, if my hands are this sweaty, I must look guilty as sin. I wipe my hand on my jeans and try to make my face into a dumb kid look—eyes wide and mouth a little open.

"Next, please."

I walk up to a lady behind a long counter. She has a little door on the counter that's open. Some of the other ladies' doors are closed so I can't visit them. It looks like we're playing house. The lady I'm visiting has a dimple on one cheek and a smear of lipstick on one tooth, and her blonde hair is put up in a snarl on top of her head except for some parts that got loose.

"My grandpa wanted me to put these checks in his bank

account. He can't do it himself cuz he's real sick. It's okay if I do it for him, ain't—I mean—isn't it?"

"Sure," she sez.

I hand over the checks. "His name is Earl Mitchell. See? It sez so on the checks. And, uh, he needs some cash—ten, no, twenty dollars."

Her dimple fades and her eyebrows run together. "You can put money in for your grandfather, but you can't take it out."

"Oh! He knows that. He just told me to try it this one time to see if you'd let me cuz he's so sick he can't come himself."

"You'd need power of attorney for that." She turns the checks over and looks at the backs. Her eyebrows have another head-on collision. "You can't deposit these checks. They're not endorsed. You'll have to take these back and have your grandfather endorse them."

What's endorse? I want to ask her, but I'm afraid she already thinks I'm trying to pull something. "He didn't endorse them? He told me he did."

"That's okay," she sez with a quick flash of her dimple.

"He's old. Hardly remembers his own name. He can hardly move. That's why I'm helping him out. Thanks anyway." I look on her nameplate. "I mean, thank you, Judy."

Her head moves back a little like she's surprised I said her name. Why would she have it on a plate if she don't want folks using it?

I walk away looking at the backs of the checks. At one end is tiny gray print. It sez, "Endorse here." There's three gray lines with an X at the beginning of the first one. Then at the end of the last line it sez, "Do not sign/write/stamp below this line."

Sign/write/stamp—I gotta do all that? I look around and

see a little writing stand in the middle of the bank and pens on wires so you can't jack them. People come up to the stand, turn their checks over, and write on them. None of them are putting stamps on so maybe you don't have to do that part, just if you want to.

I walk up to the stand and look over a short lady's elbow. It looks like she's just writing her name. Of course, that's what "sign" means. She writes a row of numbers under her name. She's about to work on another check when she looks up at me real sudden. She moves farther down the counter and cups her hand over her writing like she's taking a test and I'm trying to cheat off her paper.

I know I can't sign Earl's checks right in front of Judy so I just leave. Outside the bank three people are lined up on the sidewalk in front of the ATM. It reminds me of being at the mall with Desiree and Luz and how I didn't let Luz try the one pin number that might work. I wonder why I never thought to try it myself. Earl had trouble remembering numbers, but not names. I can't be a hundred percent sure, but I bet I know what name it is.

I get in line. A lady in front of me is endorsing her checks last minute. I watch the motion her pen makes as she signs her name. She looks at one of her own checks in her checkbook and copies a number from it onto the checks written to her. I got it! The numbers you write are an account number.

She looks up at me and sez, "You can go ahead of me. I'm not quite ready."

"It's okay. Me neither." I take a pen out of my backpack, then scribble Earl's name and copy his account number in his shaky writing on both checks.

The lady goes up to the ATM machine. She gets an envelope out of a little box. I go up and I get an envelope too, and sort of peek at what she's doing at the machine. It don't look too hard.

When it's my turn, I punch in my grandma's name: ROSE. The screen changes to some options. *Yes! I'm in!* I press the button near the word DEPOSIT. It asks the amount. I got to tear the envelope open, add the two checks again, punch the number in, say it's correct. A little door opens to take the checks. I reach for a fresh envelope, stick the checks in, start to lick it closed.

"Do you need more time?" the screen asks.

I press YES. I stick the envelope in the slot. I'm about to leave when I remember Earl's card is still in the machine and I don't know how to get it out. The screen sez, "Do you want to make another transaction?" Transaction is one of our vocabulary words. I press YES, then press WITHDRAWAL. I ask for twenty bucks. Out pops the money, the card, and a little paper. I turn around and see a big long line of people waiting for me. They all look sort of pist at me cuz I guess I took too long, but I don't care. I got a twenty-dollar bill so new and stiff it looks like the ATM just made it.

I get so excited I forget I'm holding Earl's ATM card and I drop it. I bend down to pick it up, too late to notice the curb. I keep falling forward. There's a big loud rip behind me and my butt suddenly feels air-conditioned. I grab the card and stand up real quick. I swing my backpack behind me and look for the nearest City Coach stop.

# thirty four

THE CITY COACH goes to the mall stop. Here's where I need to get off to buy some new jeans, but I can't make myself do it. Everyone who sees the back of me will laugh. I don't know how to shop for clothes. I might have to go to a bunch of stores before I find a sale, and every store has shelves and shelves of jeans and some are hanging up. The worst thing would be a young pretty girl coming up to me asking, "May I help you?" What if I don't got enough to pay for the jeans she finds me?

Pretty soon the bus pulls away and I watch the mall getting smaller and smaller. You can see the Sears sign about a mile away. We pass the big rich houses, then the not-so-rich houses, then the plain ones. When the houses start looking like dumps, the stores change too. There's liquor stores with bars on the windows, laundromats, places for cashing checks, used appliances, and a taco stand. There's Salvation

Army, Goodwill, Good News, Cancer Society Next-to-New, and they all got clothes.

At home I get the truck and drive over to Goodwill. They got a bunch of cool stuff I don't need like a Power Ranger helmet for 50¢, a Ninja Turtle cartoon video for a buck, and a Raiders mug for 25¢. I move on to men's clothing. There's not too much to pick from and that makes it easy. I pick out some jeans that are still stiff and almost new for $1.98. A pair of brown cords is only 50¢. The zipper is broke. I take them anyways, cuz all my shirts are way longer than my pants zipper. I leave the store a rich man, wearing the jeans and carrying the brown cords, my old jeans, and the Raiders mug in a bag.

Over at Wong's Market I buy little blocks of hard noodles, ten for a buck, a big pack of store-brand cookies, and chicken legs, my favorite part, 89¢ a pound. A lady spends five minutes telling me how to fry chicken. I used to think asking questions bothered people, but really most people are happy to know someone wants to listen to what they say.

When I check out, I help bag my groceries so they'll see I'm a born worker. I ask the bagger, "How did you get your job?"

He points to a little office in the corner of the store and I push my cart over there and tell the manager I want a job.

"Are you sixteen?"

"Yep," I sez, even though I won't be until July. I know I can pass for sixteen especially since I can drive. "And I know a guy who works here—Arnie."

The manager frowns and his voice gets hard. "How do you know him?"

"I met him here in produce. He was real helpful."

"Well, he doesn't work here anymore. Sticky fingers." He hands me a paper. "Fill out this application and bring it back with a work permit from your high school."

Work permit? High school? I toss the application in the trash.

# thirty five

WHIRLING BLUE LIGHTS shoot through the hazy dusk from two cruisers parked in front of my house. Busted, man oh man, I'm busted. I make a sharp right turn down a side street. I go one block, turn left, go another block, turn right, shut off the motor and listen to the engine tick while I think.

I could spend the night parked here, but then the cops would still be waiting for me in the morning. I could run away, but I don't know where to. Are the cops gonna take me in cuz I'm living alone? Are they there to impound the truck cuz I'm driving underage? I guess I got to go find out. When I walk back to the house the only cop I see is ham-face Hackett, sitting in one of the cruisers and talking on the radio.

Officer Hackett sees me and gets out of the car. "Hi there, R.D., what's up?" he sez, in his usual friendly way. He's always real nice about busting me. He hooks his thumbs over his belt, sucks in his gut. "Sorry I haven't been by to check on you and your grandma. I've been back up to Sacramento for more motorcycle training. How are you two getting along?"

"Not bad. What's going on here?"

"Some guy reported a missing person."

"For reals? Who's missing?"

"An elderly man who hasn't been home for a while. I don't know much about it. I just got here myself."

"Is it Old Man Luna?"

"I don't know. We got a call from an irate guy who insisted we meet him in your backyard. He's real upset, a little out of control, so I got called in for backup."

I notice Bobby Scudder's Pontiac parked in the driveway. Now I think I know who the missing person is. I follow Officer Hackett around the house and through the gate. I hear Bobby ranting, "I'm telling you I haven't seen him in over two weeks. When I was over Saturday, I found the mail just piling up in the box. I came around back here and I caught the kid red-handed with the shovel."

"What shovel?" I sez.

"There he is!" sez Bobby. "Arrest him."

"We can't arrest nobody without no evidence," sez a cop I never seen before. She's Mexican, but just the opposite of Officer Mendez—big, tall, built like a man, and all serious. Her badge sez Rodriguez.

"I'll show you evidence." Bobby stalks through the side door of the garage and comes back out with a shovel. He stomps over to the rosebushes and stops at the rectangle that I cleared of weeds. "We dig right here and we'll find the body, and it won't be no six feet under, I can tell you. That kid's too lazy."

"Hold on," sez Rodriguez. "We don't have a search warrant."

"You cops might need a search warrant, but I don't." Bobby sinks the shovel into the soft earth, pulls up a load of dirt, grunts, flings it aside. Dirt clods fly, one landing on Officer Rodriguez's polished shoe. Bobby digs in again and stomps on the shovel. Already sweat is beading up on his forehead and his fat stomach is heaving.

"Looking for buried treasure, Bobby?" I ask.

"You know what I'm looking for, murderer," he sez through his teeth.

"Me? Why would I murder somebody?"

Bobby pauses, panting. "For all this." He waves his arms around, at the backyard full of weeds and rusting car parts, at the blue tarps covering more stuff nobody will ever need, at the house that sags a little on one corner.

"Wait a minute!" sez Officer Hackett, finally waking up. "Who are we looking for here?"

"Earl Mitchell," sez Bobby, almost spitting the words.

"Mr. Mitchell is dead," sez Hackett in a quiet voice.

"We know that, goddammit," sez Bobby.

"I was on duty that night," Hackett tells Rodriguez. "He was dead before the ambulance even got here."

Bobby digs up another load. He holds real still for a minute, then throws the shovel across the yard. He glares at me. "How come no one told me?"

"Sorry, Bobby. Grandma wanted a quiet funeral. Just family."

"Just family? I was his best friend. What happened?"

I shrug. "He stopped breathing. I came home from school and found him. I called 911. The ambulance come, then Officer Hackett, then this lady, Leslie."

"Deputy coroner," Hackett sez to Rodriguez.

Bobby takes a hanky out of his back pocket and honks into it. He's quiet a moment. "Where's his final resting place? The city cemetery?"

"Uh, we couldn't really afford that. We donated his body to science. Earl always loved California, so we picked the University of California."

"In Berkeley?" Bobby roars. His hands fly up, his fingers curled like claws, like he wants to wring my neck. "You little moron. That's where all the protesting against Vietnam began. Cal is the enemy. What did Nadine have to say about this?" He looks at my face and sez, "Let me guess. You haven't notified Nadine."

I shrug. "We was going to."

"This is grand theft." He starts explaining to Rodriguez and Hackett. "Nadine Coombs is the actual owner of this place." Bobby tries to box my ears.

Rodriguez grabs his wrist midair. "I'll just escort Mr. Scudder off the premises," she sez.

As she walks Bobby toward the gate, he's still yelling. "You haven't heard the last of this, you little bastard. I'm contacting Nadine. She'll kick your asses out of here."

When they're gone, Hackett asks, "Is what he's saying true?"

I nod. "I know it sounds bad, us not telling Earl's sister, but she didn't care about him, only the money she'll get selling this place." I go pick up the shovel, then ask him, "What kind of idiot would bury a body in his own back-yard?" all the time remembering I was thinking of doing it myself.

"Good question, but people do it all the time."

We laugh together, even though nothing about that is funny.

# thirty six

I'M JUST WAITING AROUND in the free-and-reduced break-fast line with Scraps and Dominic, when my shoulder gets knocked against the wall. I look up. I look at eye level. I look down. There's this little rooster, bobbing and weaving in front of me. I want to bend down and laugh in his face, but then eight steel fingers jab into my chest like spikes.

"You the home got no re*spect* for *wo*men?" He raises both arms with bent wrists and straight fingers, and slices the air on each syllable.

"Huh?"

Another slice of air. "What kind of re*spect* is huh?"

"Ow!" There's a sharp pain in my ankle bone. I been kicked, but not by this rooster dude. There's another bigger guy at his side and a fat one to his other side and one a little bigger than him watching his back. Oh crap, they claim blue. There's gang signs on the fat one's binder in blue pen. I live in a red hood so does that mean they think I claim red?

Then I see her, farther back, Desiree leaning against a pole, watching and laughing with Pepsi Can Girl, who's a real joke—first she claims red, then blue, and she's white the whole time.

"You owe my woman an o-*pol*-o-*gy*, only she don't talk to *scum* like you. Watch yo back, foo, cuz you gotta *pay*." The rooster's little glittering black eyes cut right into me. Desiree takes a step forward. He swings an arm around her and she swings one around him, and then they strut away, his posse following him.

Dominic hits me in the arm. "Why'd you just stand there? We could've took him down."

I want to laugh. I guess he didn't notice the blue gang signs. I just sez, "He had lots of help."

"So do we." Dominic turns toward the wall and lifts a pant leg just high enough for me to see the glint of his switchblade knife, stuck down his boot.

"You still packing that?" I whisper, looking around. "You're crazy, home."

# thirty seven

JEANETTE AIN'T IN CORE CLASS and neither is Sterling. I pick Yeni for a cooperative learning partner and nod at their empty seats. "Where are they?"

"Sterling's mom got him switched out of this class. You should've seen her. Me and Jeanette were helping put up papers after school when she came in here yelling at Ms. Trueblood saying she's a horrible teacher, that she didn't enable him to learn."

"That's crap! Silver Boy just didn't do his work."

"I know. And Jeanette's at the orthodontist for a consultation."

"Why would she need braces? She's perfect."

Yeni twists up one side of her mouth. "You don't think she's got problems like everyone else? Ever notice she only wears long sleeves?"

"So?"

"Forget it. I shouldn't say anything." Her eyes are bright, a little wet even. She's dying to spill. A secret is like a kind of power, and if you don't tell it to at least one person you never get to use your power. "She hates herself so much sometimes, she . . ." Yeni drags her finger up her arm like a knife.

I jump in my seat. Best friends sometimes say the most messed-up things about each other. I whisper, "Why would she?"

Yeni shrugs. "I guess because she's not perfect."

Just then Dominic walks in, tardy as usual. He grabs a chair, balances it on one leg, and sits down hard. Some of the kids laugh and make Miz Trueblood look over at him. "Be seated, Dominic."

"I'm trying to," sez Dominic, "but someone jacked up my chair. These chairs are cheap, man. This whole school is cheap."

A lot of stuff is messed up in Miz Trueblood's room by now, especially around Dominic, but she can't catch him in action. She just sez, "Get another chair, please," then tells the class she's going around to check off homework.

I slap my forehead. With those two cruisers showing up at my house and Bobby digging for Earl's dead body in my yard, I clean forgot about homework.

Miz Trueblood limps up to us.

I look down at her leg which is still purple from where she got kicked the first day of school. "It still hurts, don't—doesn't—it, Miz Trueblood? Did you go to the doctor?"

She shakes her head. "I don't have time, but thank you for your concern, R.D. I don't see your homework out."

"Ah Miz, I meant to do it, for reals. When I'm at home, I don't think about school, and when I'm at school I don't think about home."

"Hmm . . . the two are completely separate in your mind. I wonder if that's true of the other kids who don't do their homework." I catch her looking over at Selwyn.

"You live in a group home," I sez, "you're just thinking about staying alive."

Next Miz Trueblood starts explaining about the Reformation and the Protestants and Catholics killing each other.

"Weren't there any Christians then?" asks someone.

"They were all Christians," sez Miz Trueblood.

"Catholics aren't Christians," another kid sez.

"Hey, I heard an airplane can't have two Christian pilots," sez Joey Barns, "cuz when the world ends Christ takes all the Christians to heaven and the plane will crash."

"Doesn't everyone die when the world ends?" asks Yeni. "I'm afraid to die."

"Are there really UFOs?"

"Yeah, do aliens rule us, Ms. Trueblood?"

"Class! Class! One at a time." Miz Trueblood always tries to answer all our questions, even the dumb ones. An office aid comes into the room with a hall pass. Miz Trueblood sets it on the overhead cart and keeps talking. I don't hear what she's saying. Nobody does. Everyone is staring at the pass.

"Who's the pass for?" someone shouts out.

"Excuse me?" Her mouth stays open as if it's holding her place in her thoughts. "Oh!" She picks it up and reads, "R.D."

# thirty eight

OFFICER MENDEZ bounces up from her desk when she sees me at the door. She's in uniform like always, shiny badge, gun, all that stuff hanging from her belt—stick, pepper spray, cuffs. A little person like her must get tired lugging it around. She gives my hand a shake. "R.D., my man. Good to see ya, good to see ya. Have a seat."

I sit and she offers me a plastic tub of Red Vines. "Have some. They're federally funded. Mrs. Donaldson is gonna pass them out to you kids when you bubble in your STAR tests. Studies show kids think better when they're chewing on something. Got to raise test scores." She leans forward on her elbows. "What's up?"

"Nothin."

"Nothing? You must know something."

I shake my head. She never sez at first what she calls you in for. She's hoping you'll tell her something she don't know.

"How's everything out in the yard?"

"Okay."

"Well, then I'll get right to the point. Mrs. Burke called the school this morning to say she saw you driving."

"What? She's crazy. I can't drive without a license."

"Actually, you can." She holds a finger up and stares at me real serious. "But it's illegal and very dangerous. If you're doing it, you better stop."

"You know Earl wouldn't let me drive. He wouldn't let his truck out of his sight."

She gives her head half a shake. "That's something else we need to talk about. Officer Hackett dropped by for a visit this morning. I want to offer my condolences."

"Oh." I look down at my lap.

"Hackett says I'm a few weeks late. I guess I should have found out a lot sooner, but I also think you should stop talking like your grandfather is still alive."

"I don't want people coming up to me talking about it and feeling sorry for me."

"Okay, fair enough. I should go out to the house and visit your grandma when I get the chance." She looks around her office at all the piles of papers, stacked on her desk, chair, and the floor.

"Can I have some more Red Vines?"

"Sure." She tilts the tub in my direction. I'm about to take some when she pulls it out of my reach. "Throw me a bone, R.D. Something was going on in the breakfast line this morning and you were right in the middle of it."

"It was nothin."

"Come on, spill it." She moves the tub closer to me. "Go on."

I take a handful. I chew and she stares. Before I know it, I blurt out, "Some guys tried to jump me."

"What? I don't believe it." She comes around her desk, and sets the whole tub of Red Vines in my lap. She backs out of her door, saying, "Stay right there. Don't move. I'll be right back."

She darts down the hall, then is back in a flash with Mr. Bowan. They come in and Mr. Bowan shuts the door. They got me trapped.

So I tell them the whole story, how Desiree liked me but I didn't like her, how she has a new boyfriend who claims blue. He thinks I dissed Desiree, so now him and his posse want to beat me up.

When I get done, Mr. Bowan goes on Officer Mendez's computer and shows me pictures of all the blues they got at Buzz Middle. "Recognize any of these guys?"

"I'm not sure. He's so short I was mostly looking at the top of his head," I sez, staring straight at the little rooster. I check out his name—Monty Sedilla.

"The important thing now is your safety, R.D. You're to spend free time and lunch in the office until this blows over," sez Bowan.

"Oh no!"

"Oh yes. It's for your own protection. And at the end of the day we'll escort you directly to the bus loading zone."

"I'm the one that gets busted just cuz I did the right thing? I ain't afraid. The dude just comes up to here." I place my hand on my waist, which makes Officer Mendez laugh. But Mr. Bowan still gives me bug-eyes.

"Then why did you tell? By any chance are you tired of fighting?"

"I can't get suspended again, I promised my grandma. So if this dude jumps me, just remember I told you so."

"We'll make sure that won't happen," sez Officer Mendez, writing out a pass to get me back in class. She hands it to me and gives me a grin, bigger than her face.

# thirty nine

THAT WAS LAST WEDNESDAY and here it is Friday of the next week, and Mr. Bowan is still making me hang out in the office. There's nothing to do sitting in the hall but talk to 504 Anger. He has a name—it's Clarence. I know cuz I hear the secretaries and Miz Donaldson and Mr. Bowan and Officer Mendez calling him that, then adding "Don't" like it's his last name. He told me to call him Lance, which I learned in history is like a big pointy stick, which might be a good name for him cuz he likes to get a hold of things like a yardstick and the window opener and the crossing guard stop signs and wave them around.

Lance sez he's sick of sitting in the office too. He told his mom to tell Mr. Bowan to let him out in the yard, that he promised he wouldn't charge kids like a bull if they teased him. Mr. Bowan said no, cuz his 504 plan sez he's got to stay in the office, it's the law. His 504 plan was Lance's mom's idea to keep him from getting expelled for knocking teachers around cuz he doesn't have just plain anger like most angry kids but 504 Anger, the kind he can't help having.

Then one lunch everyone in the office got real busy and forgot to bring Lance his lunch and his mom got real mad and said she would sue the school for child neglect if it happened again. Now everyone's always bringing him good things to eat—ice cream in those little cups at break and pizza or hamburgers and fries off the PTA cart for lunch. Then one break Miz Donaldson noticed me just sitting around watching Lance eat his ice cream, so she made sure I get some good stuff too.

Lance knows how every animal in the world does it, cuz his mom will only let him watch the Discovery channel. She won't let him go on the internet cuz it's evil, and she won't let him play video games cuz they're violent. Him and his mom raise rabbits for show. He sez he has rabbits with long floppy ears and them with perky ears and long hair and short hair and if their cat gets too close the rabbits thump and shoot straight up in the air and that scares the cat. Listening to all this stuff is better than just sitting there, but I rather be out in the yard hangin with my homies.

Every day after seventh period, I gotta head straight for the bus loading zone. For the first couple of days Mr. Bowan drove up to my science class in the golf cart and took me there, but then he decided I was safe enough walking. Usually I can see Monty, his arm around Desiree, hangin with his posse, and them all dogging me, but I don't see them at the end of school today. Jeanette is just ahead of me. She shifts her backpack and a pen drops out and bounces on the cement down around all the feet of all the kids trying to get out of school as fast as they can. I bend down and grab it up quick before it gets smashed.

Jeanette turns just then and sez, "Hey, that's my favorite pen! Don't take it!"

"I just picked it up for you. Jeez." I flip it over to her and get going.

"Wait!"

I turn and wait, the kids walking around me like I'm a big rock in the middle of a fast-flowing river.

"Thanks," she calls out.

"Kids got favorite shows and favorite games, not pens."

"But it writes really smoothly and it's all spongy where you grip it, and the point is really fine so I can write really neatly and—I guess you think I'm stuck-up."

I shrug. "Not really. You just don't like me."

"Oh, it's not you! It's this . . . place, this school."

"I guess you wish you were back in Colorado."

"Things weren't so great there either. Maybe middle school sucks wherever you go."

I laugh cuz I didn't expect her to say "sucks."

All the other kids are gone, just like that. I want to grab her hand, shove up her sleeve, and see if Yeni is telling the truth about those cuts. I want to ask her why she'd do something so messed up. She breathes in deep and pushes all that air out again, staring far away. I look at what she's looking at—Sterling, his forehead pressed against Ashley Flores' forehead.

"What does he see in her? You're a guy, maybe you can tell me. Yeah, she's cute, she's nice, but she's so like . . . quiet. She doesn't play sports and in leadership she has like no ideas, no . . . personality."

"That's why Silver Boy goes for her."

"Why?" She almost gulps the word. "Guys like nothing girls?"

"Guys like Sterling do. He could never kick back with you. He'd always have to worry if you're better than him, which you are."

"You don't think I can get him back?"

It's like she didn't hear a word I said. "Now I see my mistake with girls. I gotta get meaner."

She laughs. "Throwing rocks at girls is pretty mean."

I have to think what she's talking about. Back on the first day of school, was I really such a baby? "I was only trying to make contact."

She laughs, then I laugh. It's a weird talk we're having. If you look at Jeanette and then look at me you would think we'd never have anything to say to each other, but this is the kind of stuff we'd never say to anybody else. I'm still thinking about it when Jeanette goes off to volleyball practice and I head out to the loading zone.

My bus is gone. All the buses are gone, but I don't care. I cross the street and walk toward the City Coach stop, when *Wham!* I'm knocked in the head with a little fist, hard as a rock. Then I'm pushed from behind so I fall on one knee. *Oof*—a kick to my ribs.

Mr. Bowan is always telling me don't fight back, but I

gotta defend myself. I take a swing, but someone catches my arm and holds it. Another dude punches me in the stomach. There's three of them, Monty and two other dudes. Desiree is on the sidelines, her eyes too bright, squealing, "They're fighting over me! They're fighting over me!"

That's a joke. I'm fighting cuz I got jumped, they're fighting cuz they like to fight. I'm down on the ground getting kicked from both sides. I just curl up and cover my face. Monty sits on me. He grabs my hair, dashes my head on the cement. I feel a monster pain exploding through my brain and then that's all I know.

# FORTY

I HEAR A ROAR, smell diesel fumes. A pair of feet steps over me. I open one eye and see the bus doors extended over my head.

"Wait, wait," I'm trying to say, but it comes out like a moan.

"Driver, this boy is hurt," the lady calls into the bus.

"Can't help that. This is not an ambulance."

"You can't just leave him lying here."

"Well, tell him to hurry it up if he wants to get on. I got a schedule."

By then I'm rolling to my hands and knees. I grab the handle on the bus door. The lady helps, pulling me up by the armpits. I stagger up the steps and stand there digging for change in my pocket. The bus starts up and I fall into a seat. Every part of me aches. I see the lady who helped me walking down the sidewalk. She saved me and I didn't even say thanks. I never even saw her face. The bus lurches and roars along, its diesel farts making me gag.

The walk from the City Coach stop to my house is longer than from the school bus stop. The shuffle home is painful, but it proves nothing is broke except maybe a few cracked ribs.

Walking into the empty house is the worst. "Earl, Grandma, I'm home," I call out, my voice sounding more like a croak. "It wasn't my fault, Grandma, honest. Hey, Earl, you should see the other guys." My throat gets stopped up with something like tears.

I look in the bathroom mirror. There's a big purple goose egg at the side of my head. I can't help pressing down on it. I got two black eyes and dried blood coming out of my nose. I should wash up, but I know it would hurt. I take some aspirin from the medicine cabinet and creep into bed.

When I wake up it's dark. There's a dull, slow pound deep in my head. I test my ribs by taking deeper and deeper breaths that hurt more and more. I don't care so much about physical pain, it's not the worst kind. I think back to that time in detention when Desiree kept firing notes at me, each one begging me to help stop her pain and I didn't feel a bit sorry for her. Well, I guess she found a way to make herself feel special. *They're fighting over me.*

I roll out of bed real slow to hurt less. I take more aspirin and wash my face, peeling all the dried blood off me. Then I play a stupid game. I pick up the phone, punch two numbers and hang up. I pick up the phone, punch five numbers and hang up. I do the whole number, let it ring once. I'm about to hang up when Miz Whitmore answers.

"Uh, oh hi, Miz Whitmore. Is . . . is Jeanette there?"

"She's at her trombone lesson right now, R.D., but I can have her call you when she gets home."

"That's okay. I just need the vocab homework. I'll get it from someone else."

"All right, then. I'll tell her you called."

"Wait! Miz Whitmore! You know those Rice Krispie Treats? Well, I was just wondering, like how do you get them to stop sticking all over the place and lay down flat in the pan?"

She laughs. "Rinse your hands in cold water and press down hard. The mixture won't stick to a cold surface."

"Gee, thanks, Miz Whitmore. I'll try that."

I feel myself smiling as I hang up. It hurts my face. The best thing is to keep my mind off sad lonely thoughts. I really do know the vocab assignment, but my head is pounding so hard I can barely think. I open my binder and all kinds of papers fly out. I pick an old history paper off the floor. It's that dumb coat of arms thing. I remember how smart I thought I was, marking in four fat zeros. I flip it over. Miz Trueblood gave me a D, then wrote something I never bothered reading. "I don't believe this represents you." I get that itchy, burning feeling in my eyes.

Miz Trueblood lets kids do stuff over to get a better grade. I outline a zero with a colored pencil. Then I pick up another color and outline the next zero. When they're all done I shade in smaller zeros inside those, and smaller ones inside those. I don't even notice what color I'm using, it looks better that way. Then I shade in the boxes the zeros are in. The assignment looks done now, but I still don't add up to nothing more than zero. I stare and stare at those four fat zeros, tears dripping off my cheeks.

It's time.

I go to the phone, look at the little scrap of paper next to it, and start punching out numbers. You got to use lots of numbers dialing long distance. I don't expect them to be at Hairy's house, cuz it seems like they're always on the road, but I just want to hear the phone ring that's in the house where Grandma lives now.

On the fourth ring, Hairy does answer, groggy from sleep. It's later there than here, I forgot. I say, "Can I talk to my grandma?"

"Sure thing." He doesn't yell at me for waking him up or nothin.

I hear some rustling, then some muttering between him and Grandma, and then she comes on. "R.D.? That you?"

"Who is my daddy?"

"You're calling in the middle of the night just to . . . He was just a kid, you know, sweet and kind."

"Is that why he moved away in the night?"

"A lot of people move away in the night when they can't pay their rent. His folks were the moving-around kind, poor Mexicans following the crops. Grapes were finished around Dinuba so they had to go down to Corcoran to pick cotton, and then they had the strawberries to do in Santa Maria. He sent Yolanda what little money he could, hard-working, back-breaking dollars."

I swipe my face with the back of my hand. "Then he didn't really abandon me cuz he didn't want me?"

"Hell, no. Come grape season he was back, dressed up in his best jeans and a big cowboy hat. Yolanda would beeline out the back door when she saw him coming, but he wasn't coming to visit her."

"What was he like, Grandma?"

"Well, he couldn't speak much English so he talked to you in Spanish. He loved baseball and he'd bring you baseball cards and caps, plastic bats and balls. Handsome as the devil. That's where you get your good looks, R.D."

I let out a big sniffle, I can't help it. "What happened to him?"

"I don't know. Just stopped coming around after three or four visits. He could've gotten deported back to Mexico for working here illegally."

"How come you never told me this before?"

"You never asked. You doing okay, R.D.?"

"Just lonely."

"I figured that. We'll be out there in California around Christmas. We can all go visit Yolanda, maybe stop in at Legoland. Would you like that, honey?"

Legoland is for babies, but I like making plans with Grandma so I sez, "Yeah."

"Good." She lets out a big yawn and sez, "Say hello to Earl."

"I will, Grandma." After I hang up, breathing don't hurt my ribs near so much. "Lo, Earl," I whisper. "Lo, Daddy, wherever you are."

# forty one

JUNK MAIL—now I know why it's called that. Every day the mailbox is stuffed with newspapers, ads, and catalogs. I gotta get one of Earl's disability or pension checks soon. He used to say anyone who wants to find work can. That's not true if you're not sixteen yet. I tried knocking on doors in my neighborhood, asking if they had any odd jobs for me to do, but most people got their own kids to do them.

Today the mailbox is empty. I duck down and squint, peeking all the way to the back. It's rusted so bad I can see daylight through tiny holes in the corner. Jungle rot is what Earl called it. The box smells of damp newspaper. It smells of disappointment.

All my money is gone, but I got a whole chicken in the fridge, just for me. It used to be sometimes Grandma would cook and sometimes Earl would cook. Grandma could never make taco casserole cuz that was Earl's dish, and Earl could never make roasted chicken cuz that was Grandma's dish. I close my eyes and I can just see her laying tinfoil in the gray spotted pan. Then I remember she'd take the plastic off the chicken and run water all over it, inside and out. In the backyard there's a bush that she'd cut little branches off of and stick them into the chicken. It was to get it to taste like the branches smell. It has a girl's name that begins with *R,* Rachel or Rebecca, but those aren't it.

I don't know exactly what the plant looks like or where it grows in the yard, but I go outside and sniff and sniff all the different bushes. Here it is—dark green, spiky branches. I snap a few off. Oh yeah, Rosemary. That's the name.

Inside I put on Grandma's old flowered apron to help me cook better. I wash the branches, then cut an onion and an orange and stuff all these things in the chicken. There's a little chart right on the oven telling me what to set it at for different kinds of meat. Chicken goes in at 350 degrees for an hour. I scrub two potatoes and put them in too.

Way in the back of the pantry I found a old package of Jell-O and tonight I'm gonna try making it. The flavor is red. Grandma used to make Jell-O for Thanksgiving and Christmas and Easter, but why should a little box of red powder be so special? She put fruit cocktail in it so I bought me a can of that too.

I'm sort of excited about making the Jell-O. First you boil water and put the Jell-O in and stir it around until you can't see no more powder specks. The box sez to put in cold water, but Grandma used ice cubes. You put it in the fridge, wait awhile, then dump in the fruit cocktail.

The chicken starts to smelling so good I can't hardly

wait. I start sweeping the floor to make the time go by faster. It's almost dark cuz it's not daylight savings no more. On Monday I had to wait for the bus a whole extra hour cuz everybody changed their clocks without telling me. I hear a *ding-dong* so loud it makes me jump. I open the door. It's Scraps, his needle nose sticking out of his long straight hair, his board under his arm.

"Hey," he sez.

"Hey." I'm not glad to see him. I was looking forward to eating my chicken dinner in peace.

He pushes past me through the screen door without even asking if he can come in. His eyes roll around the room. "Sure is dark in here."

"I was in the kitchen." I lead him through the living room, pick up the broom and sweep like I'm too busy to pay attention to him. Scraps is just standing there, watching. The silence is getting too long.

Finally he sez, "What are we gonna do for Halloween?"

"Halloween?" It used to be my favorite holiday, but this year I hardly paid no attention to the fake cemeteries springing up in people's yards and the scarecrows and jack o' lanterns. It all seems dumb now.

"You think Dominic will want to hang with us?" asks Scraps.

"I don't know, I guess."

"My mom sez he's headed for trouble. All he talks about is blue. He carries that knife inside his boot. You think he'd ever cut someone?"

I shrug. When I came to school with two black eyes from

Monty and his gang, Dominic hit the button on his knife, jabbed the air, but that was about it. He still doesn't get Monty claims blue like him. "You think Officer Mendez ought to know about it?"

"You'd rat on your own homie?"

"Maybe if he used that knife on somebody." Maybe that might be too late for the somebody and Dominic too.

Scraps is still just standing in the doorway. "Something smells real good."

"Yep." That reminds me to do something to the chicken I saw Grandma do. I take a big spoon out of the drawer, open the oven. I dip the spoon in the juice and dump it on the golden brown chicken over and over. I shut the oven and see Scraps has a horrible look on his face like he's just seen his homie shot down before his eyes, laying in a pool of blood. No, he seen worse. He seen me sweep, he seen me pour juice on a chicken, he seen me—oh God—acting like a mom.

"How'd you learn to cook dinner?"

"I'm not cooking dinner, my grandma is. She had to run to the store a minute. She told me to watch the chicken."

Scraps sinks into a kitchen chair. My place is already set, one blue fringed place mat, one dinner plate, one folded cloth napkin, one glass of milk. "You live here alone, like all by yourself?"

"Course I don't, stupid idiot. My grandma's at the Palace, okay? She likes to gamble, okay? She may be out half the night, but she cooked me dinner before she left. It's hard for her, you know, Earl being so sick."

Scraps looks down at his shoes. He always looks at his

shoes when he don't know what to say. He looks up, sez soft as a secret, "Earl passed away."

"What? Get outta here!"

"Don't be mad, R.D. You been playing he's not dead long enough. Everyone knows he's dead. My mom seen them loading his body in the ambulance."

It feels too hot in the kitchen all of a sudden, but I got to stay cool. "Whatever. I gotta eat now. Later." I turn my back on him like he's already gone and take the chicken out of the oven.

"Wow, that looks good. We just had Easy Mac for dinner. That's all we ever have when my dad's working swing shift cuz it's all my little sister will eat."

"Too bad for you. Too bad my grandma's a great cook and your mom's not." Scraps just hates anyone to say something bad about his mom. That will get him going.

"You let me have some and I'll tell my mom I saw your grandma here. It wouldn't be a lie, exactly. I saw the dinner she cooked. Isn't that about the same?"

I grin real big and give him a high five. "Hey home, I think I would like some company for dinner. There's plenty here." I set another place. I pull the orange and onion and rosemary out of the chicken and dump it into the trash.

Scraps sez, "What's that junk?"

"It makes it taste good." I start carving up the chicken.

"Everything's changed this year," he sez. "We don't hang out as much."

"Stuff always changes. Member, one year we played Ninja Turtles and the next year we played Power Rangers. Every year is different."

"Well, this year sucks. I can't wait till I'm sponsored."

I serve up the chicken and Scraps grabs a thick piece of white meat off the platter with his fingers. He doesn't cut it with his knife and fork, but just eats it from his hand, talking all the time, making little sucking sounds. Grandma and Earl were big on table manners. I never thought about it before, but I guess if you got no table manners you're dissing the food you eat and the person who made it for you.

"This chicken tastes funny." Scraps grabs another piece of juicy white meat. He makes faces in between bites. If he doesn't like it, it's a waste for him to be eating it.

I notice I've only got two things on my plate which makes me remember the Jell-O. Scraps has made me lose my concentration and forget to put the fruit cocktail in my Jell-O. I was really looking forward to having the little pieces of fruit trapped inside it and now I'm real disappointed that's not going to happen. "You're not getting sponsored," I sez. "One in a million guys get sponsored."

"I am one in a million."

"Not you. You're just like me and Dominic—lucky if you can finish high school. You'll live in a crappy little house, probably not even as good as your house now."

"Not-uh. I'm gonna live in a mansion. I'm gonna buy one for my mom too."

"Your mom," I sez, shaking my head. I don't know why I gotta stomp on poor Scraps' dreams, it's all he got.

"Least I got a family. Least I don't have to live by myself. The cops are gonna find out, my mom said. They'll take you away and put you in an orphanage." He throws down the piece of meat he's been chewing on and wipes his greasy hands on his jeans. "I gotta drain the monster." He gets up and heads across the dark living room.

"Watch out for Earl's ghost," I call after him. "He died in that bathroom, so that's mostly where he hangs out."

Scraps stops. "Ain't no such thing as ghosts," he sez in a kind of scared voice.

I wait a sec, sneak up to the bathroom, start pounding on the door shouting, "Whoo! Whoo!"

He runs right out of there, no time to even zip up, and out the front door. I'm laughing so hard I gotta kneel on the floor and pound it some. I just don't learn. Now who's gotta clean up Scraps' pee, sprayed all over the bathroom?

# FORTY TWO

BY NOW I'm pretty good at getting up. Mornings are feeling frosty, but I don't dare turn on the heat and waste all that money. I get dressed real quick, putting on a T-shirt, flannel shirt, and sweatshirt. As I'm heading to the kitchen for my bowl of cereal, I see a car pull into the driveway. Out pops a short guy in a gray suit, with a pink bald head and gold-rimmed glasses. It's Mr. Deering—a guy who's been coming here for oil changes ever since I was a little kid. I go to tell him what I've been telling all of Earl's customers, that he's too sick to work on cars, when suddenly I think: Why not me? Changing oil can't be so hard.

When Mr. Deering sees me coming out of the house, he sez, "Why hello, R.D. Bit nippy out this morning, hey?"

"Yeah. Come for your oil change, Mr. D.?"

"Yep. Every three months, whether it needs it or not." He laughs at the same joke he's been telling for about ten years.

"Just the oil change and a new filter, then?"

"Ask Earl to check the air filter. Where is he, anyway?"

"Slow getting outta bed these cold mornings." I hold out my hand for his keys, a cold heavy bunch. Usually folks just leave their car key, but Mr. D. trusts us with all of his. My fingers close around them as sure as a week of groceries.

"I'll see Earl around six." He waves and walks down the street to the City Coach stop. He'll take the bus to his insurance office downtown, then ride it back to pick up his car, just like he always does.

When he's out of sight, I drive his car into the garage. I look around for Earl's orange jumpsuit and a baseball cap. Zipping up the old greasy jumpsuit is kind of creepy, like I'm putting on Earl's skin. It even smells like him. "I can do this, Earl. I can."

I grab the socket set, the wrench, and a rag off the work-bench. I lay on the back trolley—a sort of skateboard for backs—and slide under Mr. D.'s car. The oil pan is already in place. Earl always kept it in position except when he dumped it at the end of the day into big drums that he carted off to the recycling center every month or so.

I sort of know what I'm doing. When I was in sixth grade, I spent lots of time with Earl, crawling under cars, looking under hoods, starting up engines when he needed a second person to do it. I don't know why I lost interest in spending time this way. Maybe it was around the time me and Scraps and Dominic got busy building our own private skate park out front.

Right now I'm staring up at two drain plugs, one for the

oil and one for the transmission fluid. I better not get the wrong one. The transmission is a bigger nut. I also remember Earl telling me to feel the metal around it. The oil plug is way hotter than the tran plug. I have to try a few sockets before I find the one that fits the oil drain nut. I put the socket on the socket wrench, place it on the nut, and push counterclockwise.

At first it won't budge, but then it finally does. Once the nut is cracked, I turn it with my fingers. Here comes the messy part. I don't want a whole gush of oil, and I need to be sure the stream is going the right direction, into the pan instead of into my face. Most of the oil drains in two minutes, but it won't hurt to let it drip the whole time I'm at school.

Next I take the socket off the socket wrench and slip the oil filter wrench onto the socket wrench. The oil filter wrench looks like a dog collar that slips over the oil filter. I give a tug, slide the wrench off the oil filter, and remove it by hand. It's warm from the oil inside. I dump the hot oil into the pan, careful not to get burned, then set the used oil filter aside. Then I slide out from under the car, easy as pie.

My next problem is what weight of oil to use. Earl has all kinds of oil stacked on shelves, and a bunch of other parts like air filters, spark plugs, and all kinds of car fluids. I don't know which weight goes into Mr. D.'s model, but I can look it up on the internet in the library at school. I wiggle out of the jumpsuit, shut the garage door behind me, and head into the house. In the bathroom I scrub my hands with Lava, but there's skinny black curved lines under my fingernails that won't go away.

# FORTY THREE

CLOSED FOR A MEETING. Usually when the library has a sign on it like that the door is locked too, but I try it and it opens so I go in.

"You can't come in here, young man," sez the librarian, Miz Saroian. She's got gray hair and black eyebrows that shoot over her glasses when she's yelling at a kid. "Didn't you read the sign? There's a meeting of the Promotion of Literacy Team in here today."

"But I gotta do some research. Can't I go on the computers for a sec?"

Miz Saroian's eyebrows are sort of moving up and down while she's trying to decide. I head for the computers like she said it was okay. I sit at a computer, go on Google, and type in "oil weights."

I'm clicking on a website when Miz Saroian leans over me and sez, "Is this schoolwork? It doesn't look like schoolwork."

"It's important. I need to know what oil weight to use on a oil change." I type in the model of Mr. Deering's car in the search box and click. "Here it is: 10-40. It could've been 10-30. You put the wrong oil in and it really messes up an engine."

"Oh! Well! That does sound like a good use of the internet."

"Can I print this whole chart out?"

"Only if it's not too long. It's ten cents a sheet, you know."

"Now can I look up directions on how to change the oil?"

Miz Saroian looks over at some ladies who are all talking at once with angry voices, not the kind that means they're fighting with each other, but the kind that means they're all on the same side with no one here to stand up for the other side. Miz Saroian is really dogging them, like maybe she's on the other side. "Go ahead, young man. Look up anything you want."

I hit a cool website where there's all kinds of how-tos: how to change your oil, how to change your air filter, spark plugs, battery, radiator fluid, and on and on. There's all kinds of little things you can fix on a car that people will pay lots of money for. I go ahead and print out all this stuff.

"A sex scene!" one lady hisses almost like a snake.

I know I'm not supposed to listen to the ladies' meeting, but "sex" is an awful hard word to ignore.

"The foul language in this one," sez another lady, slamming down another book. "Middle schoolers have no business reading this either."

195

"I'd ban all that Harry Potter," sez another one, "if the kids wouldn't howl bloody murder. Nothing but witchcraft and devil worship in that trash."

As I'm heading toward the printer I stop at the ladies' table and say, "Harry Potter isn't real. It's just a made-up story. For fun. Nobody can really do all that magic stuff." I go on over to the printer and take out a whole stack of paper, warm as bread from the oven.

"Let me see that." Miz Saroian grabs the papers from me, places her thumb at the edge and fans out the pages one at a time, probably checking for naked girls.

I dig in my pocket and come up with thirty-two cents. "I . . . uh . . . can only pay for three of the copies today. Can you put the rest on my tab?"

"Pretty good with cars, are you, R.D.?" I'm surprised she knows my name. I thought all the kids were just "young man" and "young lady" to her.

"Not yet, but I'm working on it."

"An auto technician makes a good salary." She jingles the change in her hand. "Let's just call us even." She takes the stack of papers, puts it in her big powerful hole punch that punches them all at once if you jump on it. Then she reaches under the counter, comes up with an empty binder, and puts the papers in. "There you go, R.D. Your very own auto maintenance manual. Put it to good use now."

"Whoa, thanks, Miz Saroian." I'm out the door with way more than I come for.

Mr. D. is late picking up his car. While I'm waiting for him, I start going through Earl's cardboard file box under his workbench. There's a whole bunch of folders in it. On the tab of each one is the name of a customer and inside is a record of all the stuff Earl's done to their cars. First I pull out Mr. Deering's folder and mark the date and oil change. Then I start going through the other folders. Any customer that has a record of getting a oil change done regular I set aside. The stack gets pretty tall. Here I been going hungry all this time when I got a gold mine sitting in my own garage.

"Sorry I'm late," Mr. D. sez when he shows up. "Hope I'm not holding up your dinner."

"Oh no, but Earl has already hit the shower. He asked me to collect the money. That will be twenty-five dollars."

"Just twenty-five? Did Earl forget about the air filter?"

"Oh no. He took it out and checked it over. It'll last until your next oil change."

Mr. Deering cocks his head and gives a wink. "That's Earl. Hard to find a man you can trust in this business." He hands me a twenty and two fives. "That extra five is for you, R.D. Your grandpa is awful lucky to have you helping out."

"Gee thanks, Mr. D." I hand him his bunch of keys.

He gets in the car and turns the ignition. Nothing happens but a weak roar and a sputter. Oh God, did I mess up? He tries again and the engine turns over no problem.

He sticks his head out the window. "Getting hard to start up after it sits for a while. I'll buy a battery at Auto Mart and come on over with it. That rip-off place charges me forty bucks for installation and Earl only charges ten."

"You got it."

He backs out, a smile on his face, a wave of his pink hand.

I'm in business.

Each night I call five of Earl's customers to tell them it's time for their oil change. Some customers need other stuff like their spark plugs changed or their windshield wipers. I'm down with that, but one guy wants new brake shoes and a lady wants her transmission overhauled, and I know those kind of jobs are too hard for me.

When I first start talking to customers I get all embarrassed if I slip and say I'm doing the work instead of Earl. One customer sez something about me taking over the family business and it's about time Earl got to retire. Then I just start saying right out, Earl passed away. It feels real good to be telling the truth about that. Some customers don't want a kid working on their cars and go someplace else, but one guy slaps me on the back and sez I'm doing a hell of a job for a college kid.

Ha-ha. *College kid.*

# FORTY FOUR

AFTER SCHOOL I'm walking to my bus and a big new SUV pulls up to the curb right next to me. The horn honks. Funny how you gotta pay attention to a honk, even when you know it's got nothing to do with you.

The automatic window rolls down and a lady sez, "Get in a second."

I bend down to look in the car. In back there's a little blonde guy asleep in a car seat. Then I notice the driver. "Oh hi, Miz Whitmore. What's up?"

I get in and right then she twists around, looking for a break in the traffic. "I'll give you a ride home. Where to?"

"Wait! You said a sec! Aren't you picking up Jeanette?"

"She's got an away game at Divisadero. I'm headed over there next. I take Gladstone, right?" Clear across town she asks me a bunch of questions about school and stuff, until finally she sez, "I have a favor to ask."

"From me? Like what?"

"This is a bit awkward, but . . . would you ask Jeanette to the Harvest Dance? Just as friends, I mean. Kids still go out as friends, right?"

"Me and Jeanette don't even hang out in the same group."

"But you're friends, right? I already bought her dress. Some awful boy Sterling invited her, then uninvited her. I'm very worried about her, R.D."

"I never even been to a school dance. Oh, here's my street, you can let me off here."

"I'll drive you all the way home. Honestly, I've got plenty of time."

"Here is good."

Maybe I said it too loud cuz she sort of jumps. She don't exactly stop, but just keeps driving real slow and off to the side. "Will you at least give it some thought?"

"Stop! Here's my house. See now?"

Miz Whitmore tries not to show anything in her face, but I can see the crease between her eyebrows, and still she don't give up. "We'll pay for everything, R.D. Provide transportation. I can take you clothes shopping if you want and—"

"I got clothes."

I open the car door and she stops me with a hand on my arm. "You must think I'm a terrible meddling mother. I . . . I just want her to be happy. I know my daughter. She'll be pleased to have the invitation."

"You guys gotta cat?"

"Why no, Mr. Whitmore is allergic."

Poor Miz Whitmore might know some things about Jeanette, but not what's under her long sleeves.

That night I play the numbers game again. First I punch three numbers and hang up, then I punch five numbers, then all seven. One of the triplets answers. When I ask to speak to Jeanette, she sez, "Why don't you call her cell phone?"

"I don't have her cell number."

"Then you're not her friend."

"Then you must be Marcie or Megan. You can't be Maddie cuz she wouldn't say something that mean."

"This is Megan and I am not mean."

"This is R.D. Remember me?"

She giggles and drops the phone. Jeanette comes on in a little bit. "Hey R.D."

"Hey. Did you win?"

"No. Those Divisadero girls are good."

"Yeah? Hey, I was wondering . . . wanna go to Harvest?"

There's a pause. I'm not sure she heard right. "Just a moment," she sez real quiet. I hear voices in the background, then she comes back on the phone. "Yeah. My mom says I can. She says she can drive us if you want."

When I hang up, I can feel my face smiling.

# forty five

WITH MIZ WHITMORE IN CHARGE, I don't have to worry about a thing. She decides she's picking me up first and taking me back to their house for pictures. She comes to my door with a little plastic box. I wonder what sort of present she's giving me, but then I see it's a little flower thing I'm supposed to give Jeanette to wear on her wrist. Miz Whitmore sez I look sharp in my Goodwill navy pants and gray sports jacket, but she reties my tie before driving me back to their house. Jeanette is wearing a green dress that matches her eyes with a little short jacket. She barely smiles for the pictures and on the car ride over to school she hardly sez a word.

We're walking up to the Neil Armstrong Auditorium and we can hear the music from inside. Jeanette sez hi to a tall, pimply guy named Jerry. Then she sez, "That's the best trombone player in jazz band."

"I thought you were the best."

"I sit first chair in advanced band, but not jazz. You should hear Jerry's solos."

"I bet you're better, you just never take solos." We're inside now, and I have to shout to be heard over the music, even though she's standing right next to me. "None of the girls do. I bet you don't take a solo cuz you're a girl. You gotta be the best at everything, but then you tell yourself you can't be cuz then some certain boy won't like you."

"Just shut up! You don't know anything." Jeanette starts to walk, then run away from me. She makes it to the opposite side of the gym and through a door. I chase after her. I'm in a hallway, a part of the school I forgot all about. I think I've lost her, but then I see a bit of green material down low in a crack of a door. The door opens a little way and the green material disappears. I follow her through that door. It's dark inside, a big deserted room, with towering shapes, big objects covered in white sheets like a haunted house.

My eyes adjust to the dark. A row of large windows near the ceiling lets in moonlight. The towers are extra textbooks on pallets. There are long work tables, and the objects under the sheets begin to take on familiar forms—table saws, lays, workbenches, a display case. Jeanette is sitting on a sawhorse. I sit on one across from her.

"I never wanted to come to this stupid dance," she sez.

"Your mom told me you did."

"Well, she was wrong." She looks around. "What is this place?"

"Shop. I took it in seventh grade, the last year they offered it."

Jeanette peers through an open door. There's rows of sewing machines with hoods on, stoves, sinks, none of it used anymore. "Why do you think they stopped offering these kind of classes?"

"Most the kids I know who took shop are in double math now. It's sort of funny cuz about the only time I ever used math was in shop. You gotta figure real careful or everything turns out messed up. It's the only class I ever got a A in. Here, lemme show you something." I go behind the showcase and slide open the door. I push the button that lights the case, take out a little model of a Harley motorcycle, and hand it to her.

She turns it over. "Nice work. You made this?"

"Uh-huh. My grandpa used to be real interested in Harleys."

"How is your grandfather?"

"Dead."

She takes in a quick breath.

"Sorry. I know that sounded bad. I'm supposed to say passed away."

She puts her hand on my arm. "R.D., you never told me. You and your grandma must be really sad."

"She doesn't know. She left Earl a few months before school even started."

"But you're always all 'my grandpa this' and 'my grandma that' so . . . so people don't realize you . . . R.D., that's not possible. You can't be living alone. Aren't you awfully sad and lonely?"

"Mostly no. I got my freedom."

"Who else knows?"

"Dominic and Gilbert. At least some of the neighbors have it figured out."

"And they let you? Why?"

"I don't know. I guess they don't want to mess with it."

She hugs herself. "I could never imagine being without my family. I mean my little sisters annoy me sometimes and my mom—she's always interfering with my life—but I love them, I need them so much." She puts her hand to her face and begins to cry.

I take her hand in mine. Slowly I raise the sleeve of her jacket. In the light of the showcase, I can see four angry red cuts streaming up her arm. "See this? Don't do this anymore. Just stop, hear me? Stop. I'll be checking on you."

"I don't know if I can stop."

"Just try, and if you can't, tell your mom."

"Then I wouldn't be her perfect Jeanette."

"That's just it. No one is expecting you to be perfect. Are you okay to go back to the dance now?"

She nods and we go back to the auditorium. The music changes to a slow dance. I sez, "We're at a dance, let's dance."

I expect she'll hold me far apart, but she melts right into my arms. She's shaking some and I hold her tighter. Jeanette doesn't like me, not like a boyfriend, and I'm not sure what I feel about her, but we're holding onto each other cuz that's all we got right now. It's the best feeling I've had in a long time.

A finger pokes my back. I twist around and see it's Sterling.

"Mind if I cut in?"

Jeanette's arms drop to her sides, her eyes get all shiny,

staring up at him. She doesn't say "Sterling" so much as she breathes it.

I go get some punch and a cookie and sit down on one of the chairs against the wall, and then I go get a refill and another cookie and sit down again, and watch Jeanette and Sterling freaking, bumping up against each other on all different parts of their bodies, and I think how shocked Miz Whitmore would be if she saw her perfect daughter now.

Every once in a while I look up at the clock in its cage. The minute hand creeps from number to number. A whole hour goes by and I notice I'm getting madder by the minute. I'm not mad at Miz Whitmore cuz she was just trying to make Jeanette happy, and I'm not mad at Jeanette cuz she can't help herself, but Silver Boy . . . My hands open and close and tingle and a little movie keeps playing in my head of me plowing my fist into his face.

The music stops and I hear a girl scream, "Let go of me." It's that thing where you're yelling to be heard over the loud music and suddenly the music stops and it's you just yelling. It's coming from under the green Exit sign.

Kids start walking over there, feeling the energy of a fight crackling in the air. Monty has a hold of Desiree's arm, trying to pull her outside, and she's got her feet set and her butt kind of pushed out pulling the other way. I see Mr. Bowan slowly rising out of his chair looking toward them.

Don't get involved, don't get involved, is racing through my brain, but my feet are carrying me toward trouble anyways. My hands are knots of steel and I'm glad cuz I been wanting to hit someone all night. "Leave her alone," I shout at Monty.

"She's my ho. I'll do what I want with her."

I get right in his face and sez, "Who you calling ho? You're the ho," and all the kids in the circle around us laugh.

He swings low and dirty, but it's a wide, wild swing that gives me plenty of time to leap back out of the way, just as Mr. Bowan steps up and takes Monty's fist below the belt.

I feel someone grab a handful of my jacket from behind so I go with it, dissolving into the crowd of kids eager to watch Bowan take his heavy, graceless fall. Me and Desiree shuffle away from the trouble and go sit in a dark corner.

She can't stop laughing. "There you go again, R.D. You're my hero and it's the second time. That's the end of that gangsta. He's off to Merit Reform fo sure."

We sit around talking. Desiree is kind of wiggling around in her chair like she wants to dance. "How come you ain't with that preppie girl you come with?"

"We're just friends. She just came with me to be with that other guy her parents don't like, so don't knock her down again and throw her phone on the roof, okay?"

Desiree gives me a kind of guilty half-smile, but doesn't admit to nothing. She asks me to dance the last, slow good-night dance. It would feel real nice to hold a girl, but it's not right, I know. It would just be leading Desiree on.

All the lights come on and we blink in the brightness. Jeanette runs up to us, her cheeks pink. She smiles at Desiree in her friendly way.

"This here is Desiree," I sez. "This is Jeanette."

"Hey," sez Jeanette.

"Hey."

As Desiree walks away, her little butt swinging, Jeanette sez, "She seems nice."

# FORTY SIX

WEDNESDAY, the first week of December, is homeboy day in detention. Me and Dominic and Scraps all land there at the same time. Dominic is there cuz he's always there these days, either that or suspended, and Miz Trueblood busted Scraps on account of him throwing his pencil up to stick in the ceiling. It can fall and poke somebody's eye out, who- ever is staring up at the ceiling the same time it's coming down. Crabby ole Miz Stone busted me cuz I didn't have my homework in science.

When detention gets out, we mess around on the basket- ball courts on Scraps' board till the campus security lady throws us out and locks the gate. By then we missed the late bus, what we wanted to do anyways so we can take the City Coach to the mall. Already it's getting dark. I press my nose against the wide bus window and stare and stare at all the Christmas lights and decorations people put around their houses and in their yards. This year must be the year of the snowman, they even got them looking in on the Baby Jesus.

At the Food Court I buy us all hot dogs on a stick and sodas cuz I have plenty of pocket money. For reals, I have so much cash doing oil changes I just throw it up on top of my chest of drawers. I don't know what else to do with it, but I don't dare waste it. I haven't even turned the heat on in the house cuz Earl always said we could hardly afford it.

It's real fun till Scraps starts blowing soda at me through his straw.

"Cut it out," I sez.

He blows some at Dominic and Dominic tries to stab him with his empty hot dog on a stick stick, but Scraps is too fast for him. I'm laughing cuz it's funny to see Dominic strike and get nothing but air and Scraps flash away. Scraps blows soda at Dominic and then Dominic gets really pist and pulls his knife.

"Sorry, man, sorry." Scraps jumps out of his chair and backs away, his palms up.

Dominic grins kind of evil-like, happy he scared Scraps so easy.

I sez real bored, "You still carrying that around? I'm surprised Bowan hasn't got a hold of it yet."

"You keep your mouth shut and he won't." Dominic points the knife at me, sort of jiggling it in his hand. Finally he shuts it up and drops it back in his boot. He starts strutting to the exit, his knees turned out and bent to keep his pants from falling down. His shoulders are hunched to his ears, and he's scowling at everybody. If he was a dog I swear he'd bite. Next thing Scraps starts whining about getting the belt when he gets home cuz we're so late. Everyone's in a bad mood. The mall decorations look cheap and stupid. They're just up there to get people to spend more money.

When the bus finally comes, I pay all three fares and Dominic doesn't even thank me. He won't sit with us, but slinks to the back and stares out the window. We get out at the stop at the end of our street, still about a quarter mile to walk in the cold and dark.

Scraps slips his backpack on and jumps on his board. "Later, dudes."

"Hold up, White Boy," sez Dominic, "I wanna ride."

"Naw, I gotta go. I'm already in trouble. Your mom don't care when you get home."

"My mom? What are you saying about my mom?" Some passing headlights flash off the blade of Dominic's knife, so bright, so shiny, so sudden, I didn't even see him reach for it in his boot.

Then my mind starts snapping snapshots like a camera. It's like you gotta lay them out in a row to know what's happening. There's one of Scraps, one foot on his board, the other in midair, his balance perfect. There's one of Dominic lunging at Scraps' back with the knife. There's one of Scraps' head twisted to look behind him, his mouth wide, still laughing, thinking Dominic is playing. The knife sinks into his backpack, rips a wide opening. It's just a backpack, I'm thinking, nothing that matters. Scraps screams, he falls. His board flips over, one back wheel spinning. Scraps' eyes are squeezed tight, he's making little groaning sounds like he's having a nightmare. It *is* a nightmare, this can't be real. The knife is stuck in his back.

"Hell, Dominic! What'd you do that for? Go knock on some doors," I sez. "Get someone to call 911. I'll stay with Scraps."

Dominic looks around. The houses are dark, the street is black. "Listen R.D., we gotta get our story straight. It was red that jumped us. A bunch of dudes."

He reaches for his knife and I kick his hand. "Leave it."

"You trippin? That's evidence against me." He looks at me so cool I can't believe he's human.

"It's keeping the blood in. Wait for the doctor to take it out."

"It barely scratched him. Ole Scraps will be okay, won't ya?"

Scraps isn't answering.

A car passes.

I shout, "Help! Help!"

The car doesn't stop.

Dominic yanks the knife out of Scraps and runs, the night swallowing him up.

# forty seven

AT THE POLICE STATION they put me in a room with a table and three chairs. The light is way too bright. Maybe it's on purpose to make you feel it's no use trying to hide stuff, they'll find it. It seems like hours I been here. I told my story and a cop wrote it down, then another cop came and I had to tell it all over to him. Another cop came in and gave me dinner. I ate it without even tasting it. I wait and wait and now another cop comes in, but not in a uniform. He's wearing a brown suit and he has a big mustache that hangs down on both sides of his mouth and tinted glasses and dark skin with pits in it.

He sez, "I'm Detective Villa. You must be Richard Diaz."

I just stare back at him. I haven't heard my real name since the first grade. If he knows that, then he must know a whole lot of other stuff about me, like I been living alone. I knew if I stayed with Scraps till the cops came, I was giving up my freedom, but what choice did I have? I wanted to wait till the ambulance came, but the damn cops wouldn't let me.

Detective Villa sez, "Tell me what happened."

"Jeez! I already told you guys two times! You expect me to change my story? No one's told me nothing. Is Scraps—Gilbert—in the hospital? Is he gonna be okay?"

"I don't know."

"You must know something. Just tell me—is he gonna die?"

"What if he does? You don't seem too upset about it."

"Course I'm upset. I stood by him, didn't I?"

"He's not going to die."

I breathe in and out. "Thank you. When can I leave?"

"It's hard to say. I'll need some answers first. All three of you boys have a different story."

"You found Dominic?"

"That was easy. He was right where he was supposed to be. Home."

"Let me guess. He said a bunch of *Norteños* jumped us."

"Nope. He says the last time he saw you and Gilbert was at school. He says he took the late school bus home and didn't see you guys anytime after that. His mother backed him up."

"Oh yeah? Who on that bus is gonna lie for him? Is he gonna get the campus security lady to lie too? She let us out of the gate long after the late bus left."

Detective Villa looks down at some papers he's holding. "This all checks out with Gilbert's story so far. But then he's the one that sez he was attacked by a gang."

"He's a tool."

Somehow that makes him smile. "Why would Dominic attack Gilbert?"

"Who knows? Cuz he's mean. He was in a bad mood. Scraps wouldn't give him a ride home on his board so he tried to mess up his backpack. He likes to wreck stuff. We all grew up together on the same street this happened on."

"Do you know where he got the knife?"

"He sez his uncle Jaime gave it to him, but he probably jacked it. Ever since his uncle got out of prison all Dominic talks about is claiming blue and gangbanging."

"Dominic claims blue and lives on the Northside?"

"He's an idiot."

I say it so serious Detective Villa laughs again. "All right, we're going to release you into the custody of your guardian now. You can go home with her, you can attend school if you agree not to talk about the case, but that's it. Home and school, unless you're escorted by your guardian. Understand, Richard?"

I see he's waiting for me to answer so I nod my head. I'm sort of in shock—I barely heard anything past the word "guardian." Grandma is back? Just in time to save my butt?

Detective Villa leads me out of the room and down the hall. He's kind of blocking my view of a lady standing before him. He steps aside.

It's not Grandma. It's a woman I've never seen before—or have I? Her shoulders sort of slump like Earl's, her chin sort of hangs like his. "Hello, Richard," she sez. Then I notice it, that poop stain just above the right side of her mouth.

"Hi." I don't know what to call her. I don't remember calling her anything that summer she stayed with us.

"Well, come along, Richard." Nadine heads for the door and I got to follow her. I got no choice.

# FORTY eight

OUTSIDE THE POLICE STATION she stops to light a cigarette. I try to read her face in the flare of her lighter but can't
tell nothing about what she's thinking. The walk to her car is
cold and dark and the streets are empty. Her car is an old
model you got to unlock with a key. We get in and she starts
driving. I don't say nothing and she doesn't say nothing, just
keeps her eyes straight on the road.

Finally she sez, "You got yourself in a pickle now. What
would you have done if I didn't happen along? What do you
think is going to keep you out of prison?"

"You don't go to prison for saving a guy's life."

"I'm not talking about that. For that you deserve a
medal. I knew that Dominic character was headed for disas-
ter. Every time I get into this car and see that long scrape
across the driver's side, I'm reminded of him. What I was
referring to was you committing fraud."

"What fraud?"

"Oh please, don't play dumb with me. Bobby the boob filled me in. Earl's been gone—what?—about three months now, and you're still collecting his disability and military pension and you don't know that's fraud?"

"But I spent it all on electricity and gas, water and the phone, just like Earl would've done."

"That's all well and good. Trouble is, dead men don't use utilities. Explain that to the government." She pulls up to the house and she lets us into the front door with her own key. Of course she'd have one—it's her house. She switches on the light. Two suitcases are there on the floor. "At least it's a little warmer in here now. When I first walked in this afternoon, it felt like a tomb. I thought the pilot light was out, but the heater seems to work just fine. Don't you know how to turn it on?"

"I was afraid I couldn't afford it. Earl always said it cost an arm and a leg."

"Couldn't you use some of your drug money? I'm going to have a long, hot bath. I wasn't in this house ten minutes before that cop came pounding on the door, looking for your guardian. I told him I was your aunt and presiding guardian since my brother's death."

"You did?" The words just pop out of my mouth, I'm so surprised.

"I wanted to cut through the red tape, get my affairs straightened out, and get the hell out of this hick town. This used to be a pretty decent little neighborhood, but now it's all gone to hell. Carry my bags into Earl's room. And don't you go to bed yet. We're going to have ourselves a little talk."

After I carry her bags, I go into my room and try to do some science homework, but I read the same paragraph about matter and density over three times and it still don't make sense. I gotta do something that takes moving around so I go into the kitchen and get out some cheese and crackers and a bowl of peanuts in case Nadine is hungry. I'm just setting them out on the coffee table when she comes back.

She's changed out of her dress and into jeans and a plaid flannel shirt. She's carrying her cigarettes, lighter, and a bottle of wine. With her short orange hair wet and slicked back behind her ears, she looks even more like Earl. She sets the wine on the coffee table and notices the snacks. "Isn't this cozy?"

She goes into the kitchen, comes back with a corkscrew and two wine glasses. She holds the bottle between her knees to uncork it. "Can I buy you a drink?"

"I don't drink."

She gives me a look like she don't believe me and pours wine in both glasses anyways. Even if I did drink, I wouldn't drink with her. I don't think you should ever drink with someone you don't trust. She swirls her wine around in her glass, sniffs it, and holds it up. "Cheers," she sez. She lights a cigarette, blows smoke into the air, and looks around. "The place doesn't look bad. It's hard to tell a kid lives here alone. How old are you now?"

"I'm gonna be sixteen."

"You a sophomore?"

"I kind of didn't pass eighth grade last year, but I'm doing pretty good this year. It's easy if you do your work."

I'm afraid she's gonna laugh at me or call me stupid, but she just nods. "That's what I always told my two kids." She puts some cheese on a cracker and eats it. I start shelling peanuts, just for something to do.

A car roars up the street and comes to a screeching stop. The whole house shakes to the beat of a loud rap. Nadine makes a face, the black dot above her lip riding up some. "Since I'll be staying here, I have a right to know. Are drug addicts going to be pounding on the door all hours of the night?"

"What makes you think I deal drugs?"

"There's lots of cash just thrown on your dresser."

"That's from oil changes. I took over Earl's business."

"Earl—my baby brother. It's still hard to believe he's really gone." She pours herself more wine.

"I'm real sorry. I did a terrible thing not telling you Earl passed away. I was going to, but then the days kept passing." I look down at the peanut I'm shelling cuz I can't bear to look her in the eyes.

"And you wanted to squat here rent-free."

"I guess," I sez, but I never really thought about that. It's weird to think about paying rent on a place I've always called home.

She blows smoke through her nose. "I'm going to let you in on a little secret. You did me a favor. You saved me a lot of money."

I look up at her real fast.

"Oh, I know how terrible it sounds, but really, a funeral is such a waste. Embalming the body, putting makeup on a poor dead man, as if anything could ever make Earl look good, dead or alive, and there's the casket and all—for what? People get to gawk at it a few hours and then it all goes in the ground." She hiccups. "I got a kick out of how hopping mad old Bobby was when he found out you donated the body to Cal. Ha-ha."

"I take it you don't like Bobby."

"Not much, but he was the one who let me know what was going on here. He had a crush on me in high school, you know that? Once he asked me upstairs to his room to show me his stamp collection." She leans toward me. "Want to know what he did to me?"

I don't, not at all. It creeps me out when old people say what they do to each other.

"He showed me his stamp collection." She slaps her knee and sloshes her wine a bit.

"He sure hated my grandma and me."

"Rose. I used to think she was a freeloader, but lately I've mellowed some. She kept Earl alive a good many years. She treated him pretty good, better than my two worthless ex-husbands ever treated me. And when she left, she did the decent thing and left you behind."

I have to look at her hard to make sure she isn't being sarcastic.

"You know Earl never had any kids of his own. He was over fifty when Rose showed up. I was already a grand-mother. But she gave him a kid. Are you in contact with her?"

"Sure. We talk on the phone sometimes."

"I'll bet you never told her Earl's gone and you're living here alone."

"No. She's got her own life now. I don't want to mess things up for her."

"Well, she better stay away now. She could get thrown in jail for child abandonment."

"She didn't abandon me. She left me with Earl."

"Isn't she your legal guardian? And where's Earl now? See what I mean?" Nadine sloshes the wine she poured for me into her own glass and drinks it down. "It's quite a mess you're in, but we'll straighten it all out. Being a ward of the county won't be so bad, and in a couple of years you'll be eighteen and then you can claim your independence."

"I'm independent now. I'm earning a living and everything."

"Oh no. You've got no place to live. I'm putting the house up for sale and getting my money out of it while I can." She stands, a bit unsteady. She heads down the hall, leaving me to clean up.

# forty nine

THE NEXT MORNING I don't go to school. Nadine calls in my absence. It's weird to have an adult speak for me after I've been doing it for myself for so long. Nadine has been good enough to me, but I remember that summer she spent with us, yelling and screaming almost the whole time, and I still don't trust her.

Around ten we go visit Scraps in the hospital. At first the hospital won't let us in to see him, but then Nadine makes a big fuss at the front desk, saying, "My nephew saved that boy's life. The least you can do is let him see for himself how the boy is doing."

The nurses talk together and they get a doctor who's a lady to talk to them some more and finally one nurse sez I can go see Scraps. On the way to his room, Nadine sees a little patio where she can go out and have a cigarette. She sez she'll meet me there when I get done visiting Scraps.

Scraps is sitting up on a big white hospital bed. There's balloon bouquets and flowers and baskets of good things to eat and boxes of games all around him. I feel kind of bad cuz I didn't think to bring him anything.

"Hey R.D., what's up?" He's grinning wide, happy to see me.

A nurse is changing the bandages on his wound so I get to see it. It's a skinny jagged line, just inside his shoulder blade, closed up with seven staples. I guess with the knife going through his whole backpack, jacket, and shirt first, it didn't go too deep into his body. After the nurse finishes up, she leaves and I get to talk to Scraps alone.

"Does it hurt much?"

"Naw, the staples pull a little. Makes it feel like my skin is too tight for my back." Scraps tries to look down the hall through the open door, then lowers his voice. "I told the cops about those other guys."

"What other guys?" I sez in my normal voice.

"Shh! You know, the dudes that jumped us." He tries to wink, but his winking side is all big and purple from falling facedown on the pavement, so he just sort of winces.

"You were looking back, I remember. You saw it was Dominic."

"Yeah, but I dint tell the cops that."

"I did. I told them exactly what happened."

"You did? What kind of dude rats on his homie?"

"This is a stabbing. This could've killed you."

"It's just a scratch. Dominic was just messin. He was going for my backpack. The cops are looking for the knife and if they find it they're going to arrest him. He might even have to go to jail."

"Good. He deserves it."

"I don't blame him. It was an accident."

"Yeah? Well, then you're pretty stupid."

All of a sudden I don't want anything to do with Scraps or Dominic. Just cuz I grew up with them doesn't mean I have to be their friend. I'm sick of them both.

I say good-bye as quick as I can. I hear a loud lady's voice in the hall that I recognize as Scraps' mom, Miz Burke. She's walking my way in a big flowered dress with a man and another woman that kind of looks like her, only fatter. Miz Burke can get pretty emotional. She'll probably start thanking me over and over and maybe even cry a little and make a whole big deal about how I saved Scraps' life.

"This is the last straw," she's saying. "I told big Gilbert if we didn't put the house up for sale I was moving out anyway and taking the kids with me."

The other woman laughs. "That's laying it on him. And what did he say?"

"Oh, he was all for it. He can't stand what the neighborhood has become. With his promotion at the plant, it's time we associated with a better class of people."

I'm right up to her now. "Hi, Miz Burke."

"Oh R.D., it's you. What are you doing here? Why aren't you in school?"

"I came to see Scraps. He seems to be doing pretty good."

"The body heals quickly, but the trauma he's suffered!" She puts her hand to her forehead and sways a little. The other lady grabs her arm. Miz Burke rolls her eyes toward me and her whole face turns to stone. "Considering all that's happened, I don't want you to associate with Gilbert anymore, R.D. Just stay away from him." She and the other two people walk around me and on down the hall.

I just stare after her. My mouth feels dry, and then I notice it's hanging open.

# fifty

I MEET UP WITH NADINE and she takes me to Burger King cuz she sez she knows what boys like. She doesn't say much but I can tell she's thinking real hard about something. Her runny eyes dart around like little black fishes in a tank that's too small for them. She takes a cigarette out of her big gold bag, but she doesn't light it, she just holds it between her fingers. "I couldn't live in California anymore. All these rules about where you can and can't smoke."

My burger and fries is real good but I can't hardly enjoy it with her watching me eat. She works her mouth like she's gonna say something, but then she like swallows her words. Finally she sez, "I've been pretty nice to you, haven't I, Richard?"

"I guess." I watch her face to try to figure out how bad this is gonna be.

"Our next stop is the lawyer's. I want you to be cooperative there."

"How do you mean?"

"Well, signing papers and such. I actually don't know if you're going to have any to sign, but if Mr. Boyle says to sign, you just do it, okay?"

I don't mind doing what she wants, but I can't help playing with her a little. "My grandma said never sign nothing without reading it."

"How good of a reader are you? This is some tough reading. Maybe you should just let Mr. Boyle tell you what it says. You're not out of the woods yet. Maybe you're going to need a good lawyer to defend you in your fraud case. Who knows how many years they could put you away for that. You cooperate with him, he'll help you."

She's a sneaky one. I know it's not about me cooperating with *him*, it's me cooperating with her. She's trying to scare me. What's that vocabulary word Miz Trueblood taught us? Intimidate. She thinks she can intimidate me.

"This lawyer dude is a criminal lawyer?"

The cigarette snaps in her fingers. Little flakes of tobacco drift into her fries. She gets another cigarette and her lighter and slides out of the booth to go outside, leaving me to pick up her trash. It's like her whole life is all about her next chance to have a cigarette, and that's a sorry way to live.

We drive downtown and pull up to what looks like a big house, except there's a sign in front that sez Boyle, Pillar, and Associates. Inside it's like a house too, with sofas and coffee tables and a kitchen off to the side. The bedrooms, I guess, are the law offices. Mr. Boyle is this little old man with white hair and a white beard. He's kind of bent over so he has to roll his eyes up at you.

He takes Nadine's hand in both of his brown gnarly ones and sez, "So sorry about your loss."

Nadine sniffles and one tear splashes down her cheek. It kind of surprises me cuz it's the first time I've seen her cry. "It's very difficult, Arthur. Especially since I wasn't notified. I never got to say good-bye." She gives me a kind of tragic look over her wad of Kleenex and I look away.

We sit down in big fancy chairs in front of Mr. Boyle's big fancy desk. Behind him is a big bookcase full of books all with the same green leather covers, like they're all the same book. I wonder if he ever reads them.

"R.D., we met when you were just a little tyke," he sez. "You probably don't remember."

"No sir." I'm not used to calling people sir but it sort of feels like the right thing to do.

"It was when Earl and Nadine came here to settle your great-grandfather's estate." Estate makes me think of a huge mansion with a lawn as big as a golf course, not the dumpy house I live in.

Nadine makes her black spot jump up and down like something around here smells bad. "Actually Richard is no relation to our family at all."

"I only meant it as a manner of speaking," sez Mr. Boyle.

Nadine's lip curls into a kind of smile, but it doesn't feel like a smile. It's cold and stiff.

"Did you give me a kind of puffy candy that looks like big orange peanuts?" I ask Mr. Boyle.

"I might have. Is that what you remember?"

"Sort of." All of a sudden, I figure something out. Nadine didn't just come to California to visit Earl that summer long ago. She was here for their father's funeral and to settle the estate. That's what all the fighting was about. She was afraid Earl was gonna will stuff to me and Grandma.

I remember Nadine and Earl's father too. He was a real old guy stuck in an old guy's home which smelled of pee all the time. Sometimes me and Earl and Grandma went to visit him on Sunday afternoons, but he just sat in the sun and drooled, not really knowing who anybody was. It's sad to think Earl lived only a few years longer than his own father, but then I think it's better not to get real old if it just means sitting around drooling.

"R.D., you're here today to help us settle some serious business," sez Mr. Boyle. "Technically, I'm Nadine's lawyer. If at any time during the proceedings you feel the need for representation by your own attorney, please indicate it."

"For the love of Pete, why would he?" sez Nadine. "For one thing, he can't afford it. He's virtually penniless. In fact, as you know, he's in debt—"

"I'm not in debt."

"Don't interrupt," she sez sharply, raising her voice.

"What Nadine is referring to is the fact that when Earl died you apparently didn't notify anybody," sez Mr. Boyle.

The back of my neck feels prickly and I'm suddenly all hot. "I called 911."

"I'm referring to the next-of-kin: Nadine. You didn't even call your grandmother, did you?"

I don't answer cuz it's obvious to everybody, and I'm real ashamed.

"And what about notifying the government? You must

have had to learn to forge Earl's signature. You must know that forgery is a serious crime."

"I knew I was doing things all wrong, but I didn't believe what I was doing was wrong."

"I believe you, R.D., but the government is not the least bit sympathetic. You've got to pay back what you've stolen and there will be some hefty fines. I haven't researched it completely yet."

"I didn't go spending those checks on extras for me. I just thought since Earl was using his Social Security to support me, then his Social Security could go on supporting me cuz there was no other way I could be supported."

"You would have been right about that," sez Mr. Boyle. "Social Security would have continued to pay you benefits until your eighteenth birthday."

"They will?"

"Would have, *if* Earl had adopted you and become your legal guardian. Not even your grandmother is your legal guardian."

"Then who is?"

"Your parents."

"Yolanda Diaz and Jose Garcia," I whisper.

"That's right." Mr. Boyle hands me a paper. "Here's a copy of your birth certificate, on file at the Kaweah Delta Hospital in Visalia. Your father is a Mexican citizen, location unknown, and, of course you know your mother is housed in the California Institution for Women."

"So I'm getting sent to a group home for sure?"

"You don't necessarily have to become a ward of the

county. Granted, fifteen is a little young to declare your independence, but if we can get your mother to agree—"

"Oh, now, Arthur, I don't think that's the best thing for the boy," sez Nadine.

"Yolanda is the boss of me?" I blurt out. "She can't even take care of her own self."

"You could end up just like her if you aren't careful," Nadine hissed. "I plan to sell the house, so where could you afford to live?"

"Nadine, it's time you knew," Mr. Boyle sez real soft. "He has a little nest egg."

"What nest egg?" she sez, leaning forward. "Certainly you're not talking about Earl's life insurance policy."

Mr. Boyle nods. "I am."

"Well, I'll be . . . it's not fair! All the money we've paid into those policies over the years! Our parents bought them for us when we were teens! And this . . . this . . . *child* was just dumped on my poor, gullible brother. Earl just thought . . . well, he wasn't thinking right. He and I agreed to be beneficiaries for each other years ago." She fumbles in her purse for her lighter and cigarettes. "May I smoke?"

"Sorry, Nadine, no. My allergies won't tolerate it. And I'm afraid you're in for another disappointment. The house isn't free and clear for you to sell."

"Of course it is! When Daddy died, you drew up the papers yourself. Earl and I agreed that his half of the house would go to me if he predeceased, and vice versa."

"Yes, and Earl changed his mind in August. R.D. owns half that house now."

"This is an outrage! It can't be so. Why wasn't I notified?"

"Legally it wasn't required. Earl could do what he wanted with his property. He was worried about what would happen to R.D. when he died. He said he didn't want him turned out of the house with no place to go."

She glares at me. "Listen to reason, R.D. You wouldn't be able to afford to live on your own. You'll eat up that little bit of insurance money in a couple of months."

I ask Mr. Boyle, "Can I sign my part of the house over to Nadine right now?"

He holds a palm up against his chest. "Not so fast. This is where your own counsel comes in. R.D., I'm afraid you don't know what you're doing."

"I don't need a lawyer cuz I know what's right. Nadine should have the house. It's the fair thing. But I'll keep that little nest egg cuz I think I'll really need it."

"I think so too," sez Mr. Boyle.

Nadine jumps up from her seat. "Arthur! Whose side are you on?"

# fifty one

I WASN'T EXACTLY expecting a thank-you from Nadine, but I thought she would at least be happy I was letting her have the house. I know she's mad cuz she thinks she should have the money too. She hardly speaks to me on the car ride home and all afternoon she keeps getting madder.

She calls three different realtors to come see the house. Two of them sez the house needs a new roof and the other one sez the foundation needs to be jacked up and the junk in the yard cleared away and a new lawn planted. She tells them all that is too much money.

After the realtors go, she makes me help her haul all of Earl's files from the garage to the incinerator in the backyard. She takes the chance of getting fined for burning trash on a non-burning day, saying that would cost only a small amount compared to what she'd have to pay in back taxes if the IRS got a hold of Earl's records. I feel bad all my customer contacts are going up in smoke, but Nadine tells me I gotta stop the oil changes anyways cuz I don't have a business license.

I make rosemary chicken for dinner. Nadine pokes hers with her knife and fork, checking to see if it's cooked through. She takes a small bite and sez, "Not bad. Where'd you learn to cook like this?"

"I found out if you wanna eat, you gotta cook."

"Yeah? You're pretty smart for a guy who can't make it through the eighth grade." She taps the ashes of her cigarette into the good chicken left on her plate. She leaves the kitchen without even taking her plate to the sink. She carries her bottle of wine into Earl's bedroom, shuts the door, and that's the last I see of her all night.

I do the dishes and try to do my homework, but I can't think straight. I call Jeanette and tell her what's going on without mentioning stuff Detective Villa told me I gotta keep quiet.

"That Nadine sounds really nasty," she sez. "You know my mom would let you stay with us for a while."

"Thanks, but I better stick around here and keep an eye on her."

Sterling has ignored Jeanette since he did all that freak dancing with her at Harvest. She tells me, "Today he was flirting with Yeni at lunch. I'm over him for reals, R.D., but I thought Yeni was my friend."

After I get done talking to Jeanette, it's easier to concentrate, and I finish my homework. Later I stare at TV without really watching it, trying not to worry about what's gonna happen to me.

Detective Villa calls me to say he arrested Dominic. He got a search warrant to look for the knife in his house.

"Where'd you find it?" I ask.

Detective Villa laughs. "In his mother's panty drawer."

"That's a funny place for it."

"It's one of the first places we check. Most mothers do everything they can to keep their sons out of jail. Dominic claims he hid it there, though. He said he was hiding it for you."

"*Me?* He said the knife was *mine?*" Why should I be surprised? I know Dominic too good for that. "You didn't believe him, did you, Detective Villa?"

"Not to worry, R.D. It's got Dominic's fingerprints all over it."

# fifty two

FOR A WHILE everything's messed up. Nadine spends all her time with some worker guys, arguing about fixing the roof or cleaning up the yard or getting rid of dry rot. When they tell her what it will cost, she always sez they're trying to rob her and sends them away without hiring them. After they leave she goes into Earl's room and slams the door.

She sez I can live in the house till she sells it, but I can hardly stand to be here with her. She's got a bad temper and she never sez thank you when I cook her dinner and she's a slob too, always leaving dishes in the sink and cigarette butts in saucers and cups. The cigarette smoke gets to me too. It smells the whole house up and everything in it, even my clothes and my backpack. I've lived with smokers all my life, but now I can't stand cigarette smoke.

After Scraps gets out of the hospital, his mom drives him to school every day. I'm not supposed to talk to him cuz of

Dominic's trial coming up, but I don't care. I don't want anything to do with him. I gotta go to court to tell the judge what happened with him and Dominic. It's not like the kind of court you see on TV, it's just some judge's office and I give him my "statement" and some lady takes it down on a special typing machine.

One day when I'm in core class, Mr. Bowan comes in to talk to Miz Trueblood. The whole class is noisy, doing group work, but I listen real hard to their conversation and can catch the drift of it. Dominic's mom called the school asking Mr. Bowan if he or some of the teachers could go to court as character witnesses to say Dominic is basically a good kid. It's the first time I've heard Miz Trueblood and Mr. Bowan laughing together, sharing a good joke.

I get to spending alotta time with Mr. Boyle. He's not as old as he looks, just sixty-eight. An old back injury is what makes him all bent over, but that doesn't stop him from having fun. He doesn't wear glasses like most old people, only those little half-glasses when he's reading, which he peers over when he's talking to you. His eyes are the palest blue with white specks that seem to sparkle when he makes a joke. There's a sparkle, then a pause, and that's sometimes the only way I know he's made a joke. I have to think back to what he said. Sometimes I get the joke and sometimes I don't, but I'm getting more of them the better I know him.

He draws up my independence papers, faxes them over to the California Institution for Women, and Yolanda signs them without any trouble. Out of Earl's life insurance money Mr. Boyle pays back Social Security and the military plus interest. One day he takes me out to lunch and then he takes me to a bank where he helps me set up a checking account with my own ATM card. When I have to pick a pin number I choose the one I'm used to: ROSE. Then Mr. Boyle puts what seems like a ton of money in my checking account. He sez he'll automatically deposit the same amount every month out of my nest egg. It seems like he's actually like my guardian, but he sez he's just doing his lawyer job, acting as the executor of Earl's will.

"What about the burger you bought me?" I ask him.

"Purely a business expense. I'm going to deduct it from your estate," he sez in his all-business lawyer voice, then adds a sparkle.

I think of something I heard on a TV show. "Wait a minute. I didn't authorize that expenditure."

He taps his head and sez, "You're learning, R.D."

Mr. Boyle arranges to have Earl's truck impounded cuz I'm not old enough to drive. It's sad to see the old truck go, but Nadine doesn't want it, so I can have it back when I can legally drive. Next he takes me right down to the DMV and gets me a learner's permit. It says "Richard William Diaz" on it cuz that's my legal name. Then he signs me up for driving lessons at a driving school.

"Executors sure have to take care of alotta stuff," I tell him.

He pulls up his jacket sleeve to peer at his watch. "At one hundred twenty dollars an hour, it looks like your estate owes me another one hundred eighty bucks." Sparkle, sparkle.

We both laugh.

The way I see it, he's not acting like an executor or a guardian. He's being a friend.

One day I go over to Mr. Boyle's office to sign my independence papers, making me as free as any adult. I'll never need a guardian, but I'm gonna have a social worker assigned to me. After all the paperwork is done, Mr. Boyle takes me out to lunch to celebrate, his treat. This time it's not just for a burger. He takes me to the most expensive restaurant in town—Chef Raul's, which he partly owns. It's then that I find out me and Mr. Boyle have some same interests: good food and good cooking.

After a lunch of Caesar Salad, Beef Burgundy, and Mandarin Orange Jubilee, he takes me back into the kitchen to meet Chef Raul. It's the biggest, shiniest kitchen I've ever seen, with every size pot hanging from the ceiling and flames shooting around the sides of huge pans and about a dozen guys in white coats and floppy white hats, chopping and mixing good-smelling things. I could watch them all day, but then Mr. Boyle takes me by the shoulder and leads me away.

It's almost Christmas break when I come home from school one day to find Nadine sitting on the sofa with her coat on, her suitcases packed. I try not to act surprised. Not one bit of work has been started on the house, and she never told me she was leaving.

"I've decided not to sell the house," she sez, "not for now anyway. That makes you my tenant, Richard. I had

Arthur draw up the lease. Sign here." She hands me a paper and now I see why Mr. Boyle set my monthly expenses so high. "Wow! $1,200 a month! This place isn't worth that."

"What choice do you have? How many landlords do you think would rent to a fifteen-year-old?"

Or sixteen-year-old or seventeen or eighteen? She's got me here for a while. I guess this is her way of getting back some of the money from Earl's life insurance policy that I supposedly cheated her out of. I sign the paper without any more complaining, and when I hand it over to her she smiles grimly.

I carry her suitcases out to the car and load them up. She gives me a big hug good-bye, which creeps me out and surprises me too. I guess I've finally made her happy. Sort of.

# fifty three

GRANDMA USED TO SAY, "Careful what you wish for, you might get it." Now I know what she means. I have all I ever hoped for, living here alone in this house as free as an adult with no sneaking around and no worries someone is gonna throw me in a home. I don't know what's the matter with me, but I'm real sad.

On the last day of class we read this dumb story in core called "The Gift of the Magi." When I feel the tears coming, I pretend to cough and sneeze so I can walk up to the front of the classroom and get a Kleenex. In the story this dumb lady sells her hair—gross!—to buy a gold watch chain for her husband, but he can't use it cuz he pawned his watch to buy fancy hair thingies that the lady can't use now cuz she's got short hair. I raise my hand to tell Miz Trueblood they really need to get their money back on those hair thingies to get the watch back cuz sometimes people buy things from pawn

240

shops and they'll never get the watch back if they don't jump on it, and anyways, the dumb lady's dumb hair will grow back for free so what's she whining about?

Miz Trueblood sez I'm missing the point. I'm not though, or I wouldn't need a Kleenex. She sez literature is good when it moves us. That means when it makes us feel sad. Why would I want to read to feel sad? I feel sad enough on my own.

I never thought I'd wish for school, but on Saturday, the first day of winter break, I do. Three whole weeks in this old house with nobody but Earl's ghost. The Whitmores invited me over for Christmas dinner, but that's a whole week away. Grandma said her and Hairy would be out here to visit me, but I haven't heard from them.

I could put up a Christmas tree. We've got some ornaments and lights around somewheres. Last Christmas Grandma said to Earl, "Let's not put up a tree this year and say we did," and Earl said to Grandma, "We put up a tree," and then they laughed. Then he handed me a twenty-dollar bill, what he said a tree costs. I spent the whole thing that afternoon in the arcade and had nothing to show for it. I didn't even think if I had fun or if it was worth the money. Now I know you gotta think what you're doing. You just got to.

I give up the Christmas tree idea. It seems too sad to go to all that trouble just for one person. I walk over to Wong's and buy a turkey, a small one on sale for just five dollars. On Sunday I go through Grandma's old cookbooks trying to figure out how she used to make one. I read all the recipes for turkeys, but none of them sounds like my grandma's turkey tastes, so I start making up my own recipe by putting some things in from a couple of recipes and leaving some other stuff out.

On Monday I'm so bored, I look through Dominic's literature book for that one story about the homeless black guy named Lemon Brown. When I try to flip to it, two pages are stuck together with some red junk—ketchup that I smeared all over them. I try to pry the pages apart and some of the print on one page sticks to the other page so I can't read it. My favorite story, wrecked. I'd never do something that messed up now.

I look in my backpack for some paper to make a Christmas list, and see my binder is missing. I must've left it in Miz Trueblood's class. I can just see it in the little wire basket under my desk. I decide to go looking for it in Miz Trueblood's classroom. I don't really need it, but it's something to do. Usually the janitors wax the floors over winter break so one of them would probably let me in the classroom. When I get to school I see the gate is halfway open. There's a car backed up against the temporary classrooms. Miz Trueblood's door is swung open.

I walk in and see a girl sitting at Miz Trueblood's desk, going through her drawers. Then I see it's Miz Trueblood, in jeans and a sweatshirt, with no makeup and her hair soft and flat. She jumps and lets out a little cry.

"Oh, my bad. I didn't mean to scare you, Miz Trueblood. I forgot my binder." I see it in my desk, right where I left it. "Here it is." I go get it and hold it up.

She's taking some things out of her bottom drawer and packing them in a cardboard box.

"Are you switching classrooms?"

"No, R.D. I uh . . . well, I haven't been reelected for next year."

"What does that mean?"

"It means fired. They don't call it that, but that's what it is. Since they don't want me here, I've decided there's no point in waiting until June. I might as well go now."

"No! You can't leave us." I really mean *me*. "You're a good teacher."

"I thought I would be." She shakes her head. "You know, nearly every one of our chairs is broken. I tried and tried to catch the kid who was doing it. I always wondered how it was done. Would you show me?"

"You want me to break a chair? Right now?"

She shrugs. "What's one more broken chair?"

I look at her hard. She's not joking. "How about if I finish one off that's already a goner?" I set my binder on her desk. I check a few chairs and find the wobbliest one. I balance it on the one bent leg, sit down hard, and the leg twists out so far the chair won't ever sit up right again.

She claps her hands. "So that's it. So quick and easy. Was it fun?"

"Sort of. It was funner when I hated school."

"You *are* doing better." She flips through my binder, looking at my papers. Most of them have Cs, but some have Bs. She finds the coat of arms. "Oh, I remember this. You colored it, I see."

"Yeah, but I still add up to the same—four big zeros."

"I never believed that about you, R.D. Not for a second."

She picks up a black marker, about the only thing that can write over all that colored pencil. In the first box she draws a cross with a pointed tip. In the next box she draws a half circle and then a line with a point coming straight out of it. In the lower left box she draws kind of an oval with a bunch of wiggly lines in it. In the last space, she pauses, then draws a little oval on its side, then some short bent lines around it, like kids draw grass. She pushes my binder over to me. "There you are."

"That's me? For reals? What does it mean?"

"Well, this sword here represents bravery. Living alone like you have, all this time. Most kids would have given up."

I point to the next box. "This is a bow and arrow?"

She nods. "Because you're straight as an arrow. You do the right thing. You stopped those girls from fighting so the smaller one's head wouldn't be dashed against the cement. And you got help for Gilbert, even though you knew it meant the end of your own freedom."

"I guess I did." The back of my neck feels too hot, like I got a fever. "What's the ball of worms for?"

She laughs. "It's a brain! It means you're very intelligent."

"For reals, Miz Trueblood, you think I'm smart?"

"Absolutely. And the egg—it's the universal symbol for potential. You're going to get along in this world just fine, R.D."

"I don't even know what I can be."

"Well, now, neither do I. Let's keep in touch so we can see how we each turn out." She closes my binder and hands it to me.

I want to cling to her like a little kid and say please, Miz Trueblood, don't leave me, everybody leaves me, but of course I can't. She's just my teacher. Her smile is big and her eyes are bright, too bright, so bright I have to blink a whole bunch of times.

As I ride the City Coach home and walk down my street, I can't stop thinking how much I'm going to miss Miz Trueblood. I'm looking down at a stone I'm kicking, so I nearly smack into the diesel truck, parked out in front of the house, as long as the yard. Grandma and Hairy are on the porch, looking over the place. She hears me running and turns toward me with open arms.

"Surprise!" she sez.

"Surprise right back at ya, Grandma! Boy, do I have lots to tell you!"

# LATER

I'M DRIVING Earl's black pickup again, legally. I got my license the day after my birthday, since the DMV isn't open on the Fourth of July. That's not the only thing that happened over the summer. Grandma and Hairy, who is really Harry, got married. I went to their wedding, which was clear over in Kentucky. Harry didn't run off and leave his first wife, she died of cancer about ten years ago. Mary Jo, one of his daughters, told me he was real sad and lonely until he met Grandma.

Instead of going on a big fancy honeymoon like they could've, they came out here and spent two weeks with me. Together Harry and I cleaned up all the junk in the yard. Some of it we sold to Yeni's dad, the auto recycler, and with the money we made, we bought paint. We painted the house inside and out, while Grandma got the yard looking real nice. We didn't say anything about this to Nadine cuz we didn't want to give her anything to complain about.

"Someday she'll come down to look over her property and be pleasantly surprised," said Harry.

"Nothing pleasant about Nadine," said Grandma.

I gotta say Grandma was not too happy about me getting my independence without me asking her one thing about it, and for a while she was real mad at Yolanda for signing that paper. To make her feel better, Harry got his trucking company to transfer him to a transcontinental route from Lexington, Kentucky, to Fresno, California, so he and Grandma can spend every other weekend with me. With the Whitmores asking me over for dinner and Art Boyle taking me out to dinner, and Officer Hackett and my social worker looking in on me, I hardly ever get any peace, but I kind of like my life filled up like that.

We decide to give Earl a proper memorial service on one warm Friday evening in September, the first anniversary of his death. First I pick up Miz Trueblood at the group home where she works, then we drive over to Orange Valley High to pick up Jeanette. Even though it's near five o'clock, she's still at school working on ASB—student government—stuff. I park the truck and Miz Trueblood and I walk over to the ASB classroom. It's strange for me to be on a regular high school campus. I go to Miramonte High, the continuation school. I used to think only the bad kids go there, but a lot of the kids there are like me, regular kids who have to work for a living. We get out at 1:30 so we can go to our jobs.

At Miramonte there's also the pregnant girls and the teen moms who can bring their kids to the school daycare. I keep expecting to see Desiree, wearing her brave smile, but it's Yeni who pops up in a family way, still wearing those tops that show her belly, now as big as a balloon. She won't be going to UCLA after all. All her dad's money couldn't keep her from getting pregnant.

The other day at Miramonte I noticed a big crowd, and when I peeked in the circle I saw Dominic, just out of juvenile hall, lifting his pant leg to show off the ankle tracking device the cops make him wear, like it was some big award. I know he saw me, but we didn't meet eye to eye. I was staring at his new teardrop tat on his upper right cheek, which means he's been in jail. I walked right by him on my way to work, without saying hey.

These days the only kind of oil I have under my fingernails is olive oil, but mostly it's the garlic I press and press. Art got me a job at Chef Raul's. I'm just part of the kitchen crew, but I'm gonna work my way up to assistant to Chef Raul himself. He has taught me more about cooking than I ever knew there was. I even taught *him* one little trick— rosemary. Chef Raul came up with a chicken recipe using limes, pecans, and shallots, but still he gave me all the credit because he says the rosemary is the main flavor. Some people come to the restaurant just to have R.D.'s Rosemary Chicken. It says that right on the menu so I guess I'm sort of famous. Not to anybody I know, but when I'm walking around my school I'm happy just to feel famous inside.

When Miz Trueblood and I get to the ASB classroom, we find Jeanette at the sink cleaning paintbrushes. Her ASB T-shirt is all splattered with her school colors, blue and silver, but her bronze arms are smooth and clean, not a mark on them. She shows us what she's been working on, a single *V* drying on the floor.

"We're getting ready for our first spirit assembly," she says, her eyes shining. "We're going to have the school name clear up to the gym ceiling."

I smile and nod. While she's spending hours doing this stuff, I'm working at a real job. It makes me remember the day we built that sugar castle together and she seemed so much more mature than me, already knowing what she wanted to do with her life. Now I'm doing adult things while she's still doing kid things, so it feels like I've somehow passed her up.

I carry Jeanette's trombone case, while she and Miz Trueblood walk arm in arm. Miz Trueblood asks about Jeanette's new boyfriend, Steve, and how her sessions with her new psychiatrist are going. Jeanette bumps my elbow with hers. "What's for dinner? And don't tell me it's Rice Krispie Treats."

"Very funny. Now I'm not even going to give you a hint." When we get done with the service I'm going to make everybody dinner back at my house.

We climb into the truck and Earl is right where I left him, sitting in the middle of the front seat in his plain metal box. What I didn't understand is that after the university was done with him, they would cremate him and ship him back to me. We start driving east on Highway 198, climbing through the Sierra foothills to the King's River. The closer we get, the longer it gets between words, and pretty soon we are quiet.

We drive around Kaweah Lake and take a turn that leads to a wooded clearing near the river. Grandma, Harry, and Art Boyle are already there waiting for us. We all go stand together on a slick, wide rock that hangs over the cold, flowing water. I tell Earl how much I love him and miss him, and Grandma says some good stuff, too.

I reach into the metal box and scoop out handfuls of Earl and let him plunk gently down into the water while Jeanette plays "When the Saints Go Marching In." Her trombone sounds like a mournful old black guy with a gravelly deep voice, which reminds me of old Lemon Brown.

As I toss Earl up like confetti against the orange western sky, Jeanette picks up the tempo. She's not just playing the tune, but looping into and out of the notes, sliding down and soaring up into the echoing mountains. At last, she's taking her solo.

Earl would've liked it.